~Loves Me, Loves Me Not~

~Loves Me, Loves Me Not~

Anilú Bernardo

PIÑATA BOOKS
ARTE PÚBLICO PRESS
HOUSTON, TEXAS
1999

This volume is made possible through grants from the National Endowment for the Arts (a federal agency), Andrew W. Mellon Foundation, and the City of Houston through The Cultural Arts Council of Houston, Harris County.

Piñata Books are full of surprises!

Piñata Books
An Imprint of Arte Público Press
University of Houston
Houston, Texas 77204-2174

Cover illustration and design by Giovanni Mora

Bernardo, Anilú.
    Loves me, loves me not / by Anilú Bernardo.
    p.   cm.
    Summary: While trying to win the attention of a high school basketball star who already has a girlfriend, Maggie, a Cuban American, learns painful lessons about romantic young love.
    ISBN 1-55885-258-1   (clothbound)
    ISBN 1-55885-259-X   (trade paper : alk. paper)
    [1. Best friends—Fiction. 2. Interpersonal relations—Fiction. 3. Cuban Americans—Fiction. 4. High schools—Fiction. 5. Schools—Fiction.] I. Title.
PZ7.B455137Lo 1998
[Fic]—dc21   98-26147
                                                 CIP
                                                   AC

8 9 0 1 2 3 4 5 6 7   10 9 8 7 6 5 4 3 2 1

To my daughters
Stephanie
and
Amanda

Chapter I

The endless chain of cars whizzed by Susie and me on the sizzling pavement of Bird Road. The afternoon sun turned our walk into a desert march. That wouldn't be surprising for Miami but it was already November. We should have seen a little of the gentle fall weather the city brags about. I tipped down my *Miami Heat* cap to shade my eyes.

When we heard the bass vibrations of the car radio approaching from behind, Susie and I exchanged glances. Instinct told us it was a carload of guys out for a ride. From the corner of my eye, I could see its white hood as it slowed down when it caught up with us. Reading each other's mind, we burst out laughing.

A sandy-haired boy stuck his head out the passenger window. "Hey baby! Let me take you for a ride!"

"Not in your lifetime!" I called back, and the Blazer sped away. I wrapped my arm around Susie's neck and muffled my giggles into her shoulder.

"Stop it! You're hurting my ear!" Susie's voice tumbled through a spurt of laughter. Suddenly, her jaw dropped. "That's Zach, Maggie!"

My heart raced. "At the wheel?"

"It's his Blazer. See the Florida panther license plate?"

The brown feline on the vanity plate became an indistinct dot as the white truck blended into heavy traffic.

"I turned down a ride in Zach's truck?" I covered the spot where my heart strained to jump out. "I've lived fifteen years for this moment. Then, I blow it!"

"Keep your cool! Playing hard to get is the right approach, *chica*." Susie said, as if handing out a prescription. "This is a most difficult case!"

"*You* are a difficult case!" I elbowed her and smiled. "Oh, Susie. I'd do anything to go out with Zach. I'd wax his car. I'd wash his sweaty basketball jersey. I'd even blow-dry his beautiful blond hair!"

Susie rolled her eyes. "Now, that's a chore!"

I chuckled, staring into the distance and hoping for the slim possibility that the car had turned around.

I'd had a crush on the blond basketball player since the start of school. At first, I had been satisfied to watch him in German class. I had memorized the tilt of his cute nose, the freckles spattered across his cheeks and the confident angle of his blond eyebrows. I studied his moves at every team practice when I could stay after school, and cheered at every home game. Finally, Zach had discovered one of my talents. I was great with German grammar. Now, he searched for a seat next to mine everyday. And I lived for my daily dose of German class.

"I can't believe he borrowed your German notebook," Susie said.

"I don't mind. I'm thrilled he wants my help. Besides, to return my notebook, he'll have to look for me Monday morning." I gave her a sassy wink.

Susie bit her lip.

"¿Qué pasa?"

"Aren't you playing games?"

"I'm giving him my help as a means to an end, Susie. Once Zach gets to know me and sees what I can do for him, he'll ask me out. Call it what you want, but in the game of love there are no scruples."

Susie shrugged. "As long as you don't end up with your head in a bucket."

I laughed, giving little importance to her warning. "That Cuban saying sounds so stupid in translation. I'm not going to end up embarrassed, I know what I'm doing."

Susie laughed. "Who knows. Maybe he will ask you out."

"Do you think so?" I tried to seem casual, but my confidence soared with Susie's reassessment of the situation.

"He'll come running to you for emergency tutoring one day. I suppose." Susie drew a chuckle out of me. "Let me have a sip of your Coke."

If she weren't my best friend, I would have refused. "I asked you at the restaurant if you wanted your own drink. Why do you do this?"

Susie shrugged and dragged on the straw as we walked. "I didn't know I was thirsty then." Her face was flushed with pink, cute as the cosmetic sunburns we work on for special dates.

"Running into Zach was a good sign," I said, thinking about more pressing business. "Maybe my luck has turned and Mami has good news about the job in Radiology."

"You really want to work in a hospital." It wasn't a question.

"You know I do. The job sounds great! They told me I'd be handing forms to patients and filing records."

Susie dried up the cup. The last bit of the drink made a rude noise as it traveled up the straw. I stared at the tiny cubes of ice in the bottom of the cup when she handed it back.

"Thanks." Susie laughed. "I'll buy you another one from the hospital cafeteria." Her eyes sparkled from the sun. She had brown eyes that, like mine, were fringed with long black lashes. It was our Cuban heritage. When doling out our lot, God had granted us "captivating Spanish eyes," so her father said. But that's all we shared in the looks department.

My hair was brown with honey streaks that intensified after a summer of sun. Susie's hair was darkest brown, just a step this side of black, with soft natural waves that held any style she chose. Just a few days before, she had layered it in the latest craze. I didn't go for TV fads, but I had to admit the cut was pretty on her. She wore it above her shoulders, while mine, sleek and straight, trailed halfway down my back. I was a good three inches taller, though Susie claimed she had not finished growing yet.

"Why do you bring dinner for your mother on Thursdays, anyway? Isn't the hospital cafeteria any good?"

My hair clung to the moisture on my neck when I shook my head. I threaded my ponytail through the back opening of the cap. "She works a late shift on Thursdays. I don't get to see her unless I go to the nurses' station."

It was a routine Mami and I enjoyed. There was no sense making dinner for one. So, I bought two Cuban sandwiches, extra sour pickles on mine. I took one to Pediatrics for Mami, then we ate together as I told her about my plans for the weekend. On my way out, I always peeked in the newborn nursery window.

4

A blast of cool air greeted us as we entered the hospital lobby. I hooked my finger in the neck of my T-shirt and vented out the heat. I waved to the evening receptionist, then pressed the elevator button for the third floor.

"I can't understand how you can enjoy eating here." The corners of Susie's mouth turned down in disgust. "Hospitals smell of medicines and disinfectants."

"It doesn't bother me. You either like hospitals or you don't." I shrugged. "I feel very comfortable here. Besides, I look forward to my time with Mami."

"Are we going to make the basketball game tomorrow night?" Susie watched the changing electronic numbers.

"Sure, unless Mami says they want me to start work right away."

I had dreamed of working in the hospital since I was a child. I wanted to be useful to patients and help them feel better. Mami was happy as a nurse. I knew I'd follow in her footsteps when I finished high school.

As the door slid open, I could see Mami in the glassed-in room behind the nurses' station, where medicines were kept. She wore a yellow smock with Noah's arks and smiling animals printed on it. It was my favorite. She had a variety of smocks, but hospital regulations required nurses to wear white pants and shoes. Her straight dark hair curved under, framing her pretty face as she concentrated. She was measuring colorful syrup into tiny plastic cups on a tray. She didn't see us, so I tapped on the glass.

"Maggie!" Mami's face shone. She stepped out and planted a kiss on my cheek. She kissed Susie too. It was the customary Cuban mother's greeting. "I'm glad you're here."

"I brought you flan for dessert," I said, raising the white paper bag as proof.

"All those calories and cholesterol!" Mami shook her head, but she winked her eye with an impish smile. She loves Cuban egg custard.

As I left the house in the morning, I had plucked the petals from a jasmine to figure out my fortune for the day. It was a habit I'd grown used to on the way to school. This morning I'd wanted to find out if I'd get the job. I called out sí to every other petal, and I'd been pleased when the final one was another sí. Surely, it was a sign of the result of my job interview. Still, I couldn't help feeling anxious. "Did I get the job?"

"I have to pass around my six o'clock medications. Why don't you show Susie the newborns and I'll take a few minutes with you after."

"Spare me the agony, Mami."

Mami arranged the teeny cups in a straight line, avoiding my eyes. "We'll talk about it when I finish."

I didn't care how sour I sounded. "I didn't get it. I can tell."

Susie's attention was taken up by a speck on the floor.

"It's not as simple as that, *mi vida*," Mami said. "Let me finish my work and we'll talk."

"Same old story! They won't hire me because I have no experience and I have no experience because they won't hire me."

Mami looked at me sadly. I hadn't meant to raise my voice, but Dottie, one of Mami's co-workers, piped in, without taking her eyes off the computer screen: "Life's tough, sweetie."

I took Susie to the newborn nursery window. She pressed her forehead against the glass and drooled over the babies for a few minutes. The quiet babies were the cutest, she assured me. I

6

leaned against the wall. I didn't feel like looking in. I liked the screamers. I felt like crying along with them.

I had been so sure that I'd get a job. The jasmine had predicted good things for me today. My morning fortune was usually on the mark. My eyes stung from anger.

Susie and I bought two Cokes at the cafeteria and brought back a decaff Diet Coke for Mami. I'll never understand how she can drink that stuff! Ancient magazines lay scattered on the coffee table of the third floor waiting room. We took over the empty peach and aqua room. It seemed every hospital was decorated in Florida colors these days, with beach scenes on the walls and ginger jars stuffed with seashells, as if concerns about sick relatives could be forgotten by pretending to relax by the sea.

"I can get you a job at the grocery store," Susie offered.

"Bagging food doesn't get me any closer to patients. Thanks anyway."

"It's your loss, *chica*." Susie shrugged. A sliver of trim midriff showed for a moment under her lime green cropped T-shirt. "You'll miss out on the cute guys that show up at the store. They don't come in here for X-rays very often."

"The jocks do! When they get hurt."

"Let me get this straight." She leaned forward and stared into my eyes. "You want to work in the hospital in case Zach breaks a bone?"

She knew better. But she got me to smile in spite of my disappointment. "Think about it. The job includes slipping off his clothes, so we can X-ray him."

Susie batted her lashes. "Where do I go to apply?"

I laughed. "I spotted him first. He's all mine." It was an unspoken rule. Friends didn't set their sights on the same prey.

Whoever aimed first had first rights to the guy. Though Zach was far from being mine.

"I hope my sandwich is still warm," Mami said, taking the chair next to mine. Despite years of living in Miami, she spoke English with a strong Spanish accent. Though we peppered our talks with words in Spanish, we usually spoke in English when we were at the hospital. Many of the people she worked with spoke only English. She popped open her Diet Coke and spread her sandwich wrapper on a blue tray she brought from her station.

"What did the personnel guy say?"

"Mr. Ortega, Maggie," Mami corrected.

"Whatever."

Susie bit back a smile.

"He was impressed with the letters from your teachers. He says I should be proud they think so highly of you. I told him I already am." Mami gave me one of her 'My, but-you-have-grown' smiles.

She was trying to ease my disappointment. Her patronage irritated me. "Get down to business, Mami."

"He thinks you're too young." Crusty chips of Cuban bread rained down on the tray when Mami took a bite.

"I can do the work."

"You are fifteen. They've never hired anyone that young."

I set my can of Coke on the table. "So I wasted my time coming in."

"Sitting through an interview is a valuable experience. You'll know what to expect when you apply for jobs in the future."

"I wasted his time, then."

8

"You've made a good impression, Maggie. Mr. Ortega will think of you in the next few years, when there's an opening you can handle."

"I bet he told you I could volunteer."

Mami nodded.

Susie gave her a commiserating smile. I hated it when they teamed their sympathy.

"I explained to him you've been helping out for years."

"When you get no paycheck, no one takes you seriously." I got up and leaned on the windowsill. The traffic on the road was less frantic, now that rush hour was over.

"Dr. Stevens does."

I raised an eyebrow. "Papi's old friend?"

Mami gave me a mysterious smile and took a bite of her sandwich to drag out the suspense. I stared until she finished munching. She patted her lips with a napkin. I could tell she enjoyed making me wait.

"He thought of you first. He thinks you're just right for a job he has."

"Doing what?" My confidence in the divining power of the jasmine returned. Mami had me sitting on the edge of my chair.

"He has an elderly patient who broke her leg a couple of months ago. Now she has trouble standing for very long. Mrs. Maxwell—that's the lady's name—needs someone to come by every day."

I'd miss out on watching Zach on the courts. But Mami had sparked my curiosity. "What kind of help does she need?"

"She's looking for a companion who can run to the store for bread and milk, help her fold laundry, or simply take a walk with her."

"They'll pay me, right?"

"Of course. Dr. Stevens will give you the nursing referral, but Mrs. Maxwell will be your employer."

The job sounded very good, but when she called it a nursing referral I was hooked.

Mami must have read the interest in my eyes. "Here's Mrs. Maxwell's address and phone number. Stop by her house Saturday and let her meet you. Then, I'll call Dr. Stevens and let him know if you'll take the job."

Before I dialed, I prepared for my phone call to Mrs. Maxwell, rehearsing for a few minutes what I would say. Yet, as always happened when I had a lot at stake and was nervous, my Spanish accent came through on the phone. Mrs. Maxwell was pleased I had called and invited me over right away.

She lived a block and a half from my home, in a white masonry house with black shutters and an intricate wrought-iron railing on the front porch. She was one of the original homeowners in the area, now represented by a handful of gray-haired, English-speaking retirees who clung to their solid little homes and a world of memories. Our modest neighborhood, just outside the posh city of Coral Gables, had been a popular place to raise children in the 1950s, when the pace of life was slower and kids' shouts rang out only in English. The new generation of homeowners had been born on foreign soil and spoke with a multi-hued palette of sounds. They planted roots where their modest earnings allowed and moved on to modern high-ceilinged houses on tiny lots further west, when their fortunes improved.

Mami was proud to own our little two-bedroom house, with its big yard and barrel tile roof. It was big enough for the two of us. Our home was close to good schools and to her job. And our neighbors, mostly Cuban families, were decent and hard working.

I waited a few minutes for Mrs. Maxwell to answer the doorbell. She had warned me that she didn't get around as fast anymore, so I had time to notice that the potted plants on the porch were wilted, some of them beyond help.

"Hello, Maggie," she said. "I hope I didn't keep you waiting very long."

Mrs. Maxwell's hair didn't have a trace of color. Her short bob was a dazzling white. Her eyes were palest blue and the corners crinkled when she smiled.

"Oh, not at all," I said shyly.

"Come in. I'll get you something cold to drink."

The furniture in the living room was dark with glossy marble tops on the side and coffee tables. When Mami filled me in on her early years in Cuba for my cultural enrichment she'd described, with a wistful sheen in her eyes, her grandmother's parlor. It was a spacious room with Moroccan tile floors and wood-shuttered windows, and it was filled with antiques. I pictured a childlike version of Mami playing jacks on the cold stone of the coffee table, the best material for a sharp rebound of the little rubber ball. Mrs. Maxwell's home did not have tile floors. Instead, a blue-flowered Oriental rug covered the luster of golden oak planks. I doubted the six chairs around the dark dining room table had been used in a while. Mrs. Maxwell lived alone. And I was sure the china and crystal in the glass breakfront had not served guests for many years.

I followed Mrs. Maxwell into the kitchen.

"Dr. Stevens tells me your mother is a nurse at the hospital." She filled two glasses with ice and reached in the refrigerator for a bottle of ginger ale.

"She went back to college and got her degree," I said, helping her unscrew the plastic bottle top.

"It takes a lot of determination to do that, when you have a family." Mrs. Maxwell handed me a glass and a paper napkin. "Let's go to the Florida room. It's my favorite place to sit in the morning."

I could see why. The room was bathed in light filtered through tropical fruit trees and streaming in through a bank of windows. She pointed to the cushioned wicker sofa for me and took a seat on the matching chair.

"I figured you'd know how to handle patients too."

"My mother works with children. I don't think she's ever had patients who were . . ." A wave of heat rose to my face as I tried to find a word that would be inoffensive. ". . . adults."

Mrs. Maxwell smiled.

"I don't think my mother has ever taken care of patients at home either."

"Well, I'm not much of a patient. As you can see, I get around very well. I travel at a slower pace these days, that's all. Dr. Stevens and my daughter are conspiring to keep close watch on me." She leaned forward as though she shared a special secret with me. "I've been thinking maybe it's not such a bad idea."

"I heard you broke your leg." My gaze darted to her calves before I could stop.

But Mrs. Maxwell raised the hem of her dress just above the knee and patted her right leg. "I fell down by the avocado tree. I must have tripped over a root." A small dimple appeared in the center of her chin when she thrust it in the direction of the tree. "It took me a long time to make my way back into the house and reach the phone. My daughter wasn't planning to stop by that day. Her children keep her so busy with their activities. It would have been evening before my neighbors arrived from work and spotted me lying in the yard."

"That sounds awful!"

"It was tough. But the worst part was staying with my daughter's family and not being able to swim in their pool." Mrs. Maxwell laughed.

"That must have been frustrating." I looked around, wondering if she wanted me to start work today. Terra-cotta pots were grouped by the bank of windows, on benches and on the tile floor. The soil in them was dry as a January lawn. "What kind of help do you need?"

"Darling, all I want is a little companionship."

"Would you like me to water your plants?"

"That's the kind of help I'm looking for!" She got up and showed me where she kept the watering can. I filled it at the faucet just outside the Florida room door.

"I can't drive anymore and I don't get to see my friends very often. And my grandchildren!" She looked up to the heavens. "They don't seem to find the time to visit anymore. My oldest grandson can drive now. When he doesn't have practice after school, you'd think he'd stop by sometimes. But I hardly ever see him." She gave me a mischievous look. "Do you visit your grandmother often?"

I was glad I could be honest. "I can't. She lives in Chicago with my aunt and uncle."

"That's too bad. I know that many Cuban families are scattered all over the country. Will you see her for the holidays?"

"No, not this year. We can't afford to travel often. But we talk on the phone and I write to her." I propped up a wilted philodendron.

"I think we can make it come back to life," she said. "I can't bend down to fill the can any longer and I've neglected my plants."

"Your angel-wing begonia is about to bloom. If we don't keep it moist, it will shed its buds."

Mrs. Maxwell's eyebrow rose. "How do you know so much about plants?"

I smiled and headed out for a refill of the can. "I've always loved plants. I have a few of my own."

"That's unusual for a girl your age."

I shrugged. "I work in the yard with my mother. It's a good way to get a tan! I'll go water the pots on the front porch."

A hint of a smile brightened her face. As I ran around the side of the house, I heard her murmur, "I think we'll get along just fine."

Chapter 2

For years, Mami had pampered the jasmine vine that wrapped around the ornamental wrought iron on our front porch. Its fragrant blossoms flowered year round, though they were at their best in spring and fall. Mami said her family had grown a similar jasmine in her childhood garden in Cuba and she wanted a reminder of those carefree times.

She said it was called Arabian jasmine, a name which inspired me with exotic and mystical notions. I had come to associate the plant with ancient stories she'd read to me years before while sitting on the front steps. My mother's voice had filled the evenings with tales of magic and divining powers. As she described the scents of herbs, incense and spices which perfumed that part of the world in old times, the breeze swirled the jasmine's sweet fragrance around us.

I played with the notion that the tiny flowers could predict my daily fortune. So, as I stepped out on my way to school each morning, I picked a full white blossom. I could guess the outcome of an important event by calling out *sí ó no* as I plucked each petal. My day's fortune lay on the final petal.

Though I relied on the power of the jasmine, I had kept the notion to myself. I was afraid Susie would laugh at me. Lately, instead of wondering about the result of school tests or the possibility of getting a job, I put my efforts on guessing Zach's feelings for me. I found that on days when my fortune pointed against me, our meetings were lifeless as a geometry lecture. On days when the last petal suggested that he loved me, fireworks of excitement flared between us.

Today, the final petal said he loved me.

While hurrying down a hallway as I got to school, my friend Conchi called to me, "*¡Oye!* Listen!" Her Jantzen backpack, filled with books, dangled by one strap from her chubby arm. "Some kid is asking about you!"

"Who's that?"

"I don't know his name." Conchi had a knack for knowing just enough to entice and not enough to prove she was plugged in. She gave me a side glance and a knowing grin. "He's tall, blond, a high scorer, if you ask me."

A tingle of excitement ran through me. "Was it the guy on the basketball team?"

"Now really! How would I know?" Conchi's family claimed to trace their roots to Spanish aristocracy, though it did them little good living in exile from Cuba. Her parents were very particular about the activities she could attend, and school games were one of those forbidden gatherings. Her mother insisted on chaperoning her everywhere and I figured she just didn't like sports.

"What was he wearing?" I wouldn't permit myself to dream that it might have been Zach. Not yet. I wanted proof.

"Pants and a shirt. *Really*, Maggie. If a cute guy calls you over, even if it's to ask about your friend, is your mind going to zero in on his clothes?"

"Was he carrying a notebook?" I asked, reading her pudgy face with interest.

"Maggie, everyone packs notebooks in school. Of course he was." She put a hand on my arm and gave me a teasing wink. "He had more than an interest in class notes. He even asked what lunch session you're assigned."

My heart skipped a beat. "You point him out when you see him again. I gotta run. I have to make it to my locker before the second bell rings."

Opening the combination lock I was given this year was tough. I might as well be cracking a dried out coconut with a bare fist. I couldn't remember if it was twenty-three to the left or to the right and it took me a few tries every day to get the locker open. The few minutes between second and third period were the most convenient to switch books, even if it was just before German class. None of my other classrooms were in the same hallway as the bank of lockers. So I worked fast to avoid missing a minute of the only class I shared with Zach.

The innards clicked when I turned the numbered dial. I jerked down the lock, but it didn't give. "*¡Caramba!*" I was losing precious seconds of contact with Zach.

"I'll give you a hand."

My heart sent a rush of blood through my body and stopped. Zach's voice had the power to rearrange the timing of my clock. *¡Dios mío!* Had I been thinking out loud? Had he heard my thoughts?

17

"Hey!" I said coolly. Another great achievement, Maggie! Try to sound unperturbed.

He rolled the dial a few times to get a clean start. A little dimple appeared on his chin when he concentrated. I had an urge to touch my finger to it. But I knew better.

"I've been looking for you this morning," he said.

I had my proof. Suddenly I couldn't meet the look from his pale blue eyes. "I've been around."

"What's your number?"

He wanted my phone number! I had waited so long for this moment. "Five, five, five, three, three, eight, two. Don't you want a pencil to write it down?"

The straight line of his brow scrunched and he gave me a perplexed look. "That's the combination to your lock?"

Stupid! I had rushed things. I was sure the crimson on my face pulsed like a UFO on a dark sky. I called the three double-digit combination slowly, as he turned the knob. The lock clicked free. The metal door creaked as it swung open, and I worried that I had not cleaned out all the heart-covered notes Susie passed to me.

"I gotta hand your notebook back before I go in to class. Mrs. Berger would yell like a storm trooper if she knew you'd let me use it." He leaned against the turquoise lockers. His yellow piqué golf shirt drooped slightly past his wide shoulders. His khaki Dockers fit just right. Conchi might get too distracted to check out a boy's clothes. But I enjoyed an eyeful of Zach's body any time.

"Yeah, that would get her all worked up." My hand fumbled around the crowded metal box while I tried to remember all the books I'd need until lunch. My memory went out to pasture while I was around him. I knocked aside the paper bag that carried a sandwich from home and it tumbled out of the locker. Zach caught it in mid-air.

"You bring lunch from home?"

I was mortified. I didn't want him to think I was a dork for doing it. "I hate cafeteria food." I lied. I like their pizza. I like their chicken patties. I love their pasta salads.

"Me too. I run over to The Spigot for fast food." He flashed me a peek of his tenth grade ID inserted in the pages of his German textbook.

I made a mental note. Susie and I would have to run over to The Grill and Spigot for burgers. Only freshmen were kept on campus. Our sophomore IDs, which gave us the authority to leave the school grounds, were going to waste.

"What've you got in here?" Zach peered into the paper bag before I could snatch it away. "Cuban girls bring the weirdest lunches! Tuna salad . . . plantain chips . . . Yuck! Those things don't go together."

"Says who?" I took the bag from his hands, folded shut the top and threw it back into the locker.

He laughed. "Let's go in. I want to get a seat next to you."

I led the way into class, my face beaming.

German class was the shortest hour of the day. I was sure the school was cheating me of my allotted time with Zach. Geometry, the class that followed, was awarded those extra minutes. That was the longest period of the day. I was sure it was in part because my stomach grumbled for lunch, which came next.

But mostly it was due to the anticipation of breaking the news about Zach to Susie when I joined her.

I arrived at the cafeteria before she did, bought a drink and a fruit cup and took an empty picnic table in the courtyard. I couldn't bring myself to dump out my tuna sandwich, but I would have preferred a hamburger across the street for the chance to run into Zach. Our outing for fast food would have to wait. I didn't carry enough money for a full lunch. Besides, it would be too obvious to show up at The Spigot on the same day Zach told me that's where he hangs out.

"Hey, Mag!" Carlos Cepero set down a heaping tray of food next to mine. "You look like you want company."

"Actually, no." I looked him over from head to toe, but granted him a smile. "I'm waiting for a friend."

I must have given him mixed signals, though Carlos needed little encouragement, because he straddled the bench next to me. His friend set down his lunch and sat on the opposite bench.

"Mag, this is Just." Carlos shortened everyone's name. It gave the impression you were his closest friend.

"Hi, Just," I said, unhappy they'd installed themselves at my table. I was looking forward to private time with Susie.

"Justin, Justin Bentley," the tall boy said. His tawny hair was a few inches long on top and closely cropped on the back and sides. A small silver ring hung from his left earlobe. He wasn't a bad looker, I just didn't care to look his way.

"I'm Maggie Castillo."

"Yeah, I know," he mumbled. His face had a fresh wash of crimson that I didn't think I'd detected before. He brought the plate of spaghetti and meatballs closer to him, salted his French fries and pushed aside the two guava pastries. "I've seen you around."

His admission made me uncomfortable, perhaps because I'd never noticed him before. I glanced at Carlos and changed the subject. "If it was up to you, Carlos, everyone would have a one-syllable name."

He tossed back his nut-brown hair with a motion of his head. It was longer since I'd last noticed. "Sure, it's a time saver. If I used your full name, the bell would ring before I was through, Margarita."

In spite of myself, I chuckled. I hadn't seen much of Carlos this year. His dark expressive eyebrows gave life to his words, like punctuation improves the written word. A grayish haze lined his jaw and upper lip. I was sure that now he was using a razor every morning.

"You still walking every day?" Carlos asked.

"Whenever I can." I got busy with my fruit salad.

"Mag's trying out for the next Olympics," Carlos informed Justin. "Brisk walking. It's a new sport."

Justin's lips broke into an open grin. I shook my head, but the boy's smile was contagious, and I couldn't help returning it.

"You've gotta keep at it, Mag," Carlos went on. "Can't let up. You'll get out of shape and lose your edge."

"I'm working now. I don't always have the time."

"What do you do?" Justin asked.

"I take care of an elderly patient." I looked around for Susie. To my disappointment, she was caught in the long line for snacks. I couldn't wait for her to rescue me from these two.

Justin's fork hovered in mid-air for a moment. "You're a nurse?" He popped the meatball in his mouth.

I didn't feel like explaining. "Something like that."

There was a long pause. These two won the prize for persistence. But I wasn't about to award it. I wished they would move along.

"Just's in my physics class. We have math together, too. With Mr. Sutter."

"Yes, I know. Mr. Skinny Tie."

Carlos laughed. An unsure smile tilted the corners of Justin's mouth, but I could tell he didn't know the story behind the nickname.

"Someone's got to work up the nerve to tell him his collection of ties is out of date," Carlos said.

"I hope you don't." I gave him a warning look. "He may be boring, but he's a pretty decent teacher. It would hurt his feelings."

I broke the tab on my Orange Crush. I couldn't fathom why Carlos had chosen to sit with me today, the one time I wanted Susie all to myself.

"Just's new at Glades Ridge this year."

"Oh?" I arched a brow and took a bite out of my tuna sandwich. I had pressing things on my mind. I wished they'd find someone else to bug. "Have you made any friends yet?"

"He's trying to, Maggie." Carlos gave me an icy glance. "I need some ketchup. I'll be back."

"I don't think I've seen you before," I said, embarrassed that my message had been received after all.

"I've seen you, in the halls and stuff. Don't you have algebra with Mr. Sutter the period before this one?"

"Geometry." If he wanted a conversation with me, he'd chosen the wrong subject. "It's my most boring class."

"Maybe that's because I'm not in it!" He gave me a crooked smile.

"I don't think anyone can make geometry interesting. Sorry!"

Conchi had been headed to my table, but suddenly opened her eyes wide and gave me a thumbs-up. Then she turned and sat with a few Cuban girlfriends, who put their heads together as if in a huddle. The girls glanced in our direction with approval. I guessed she told them Zach had been looking for me this morning. Either that, or she was impressed that yet another boy was sitting with me.

"Look at it as though it were a puzzle."

"What?" I asked, looking back at him.

"Math's a puzzle with a piece missing." His eyes were the same green as forest moss. "Only one answer will fit."

That put a different spin on the subject. "I never heard that before."

"It's a challenge to solve the puzzle, but that's what makes it interesting." He took a gulp of his Coke. "How are you doing in the class?"

I shrugged. I wasn't going to let a total stranger know that it was my poorest grade. "All right. I suppose."

"Let me know if you want help."

I wanted to tell him I didn't.

"The line took forever," Susie said, putting her food on the table next to me.

"I'm Justin Bentley." He gave Susie a nod.

"This is Susie Domínguez, my best friend." I had to be polite.

Susie questioned me with her eyes, raising a leg over the bench and trying to appear graceful at it. I answered with a discreet shrug.

"Justin's new this year," I started to explain awkwardly.

"Hey Suze!" Carlos came up behind her and pinched Susie playfully. I was glad to be relieved of the burden of conversation.

"Hey Carlos! I haven't seen much of you lately." Susie had that twinkle in her eye that she reserved for special boys on her list.

"You haven't looked. I've been around." Carlos dropped a handful of ketchup packets in front of Justin. "I see you've met Just. *Buena gente.* He's good people!"

"I've got something to tell you," I whispered to Susie.

"Where did you go to school before?" Susie asked.

"He went to Masterson's last year," Carlos answered, not giving Justin a chance. His eyes were glued on Susie.

"Ooh!" She made the sound trail teasingly. "Private school material."

Justin brushed off the comment. "I'm here now."

"I can't wait to tell you what I found out this morning!" I whispered again.

"Later," Susie mouthed, not taking her eyes off Carlos.

Carlos touched the tip of his thumb to his pointer and puckered his lips. "Justin's an ace in math."

Susie laughed. "Like you?"

"Like me." Carlos stared into her eyes. "My two great loves: Math and Susie Domínguez!"

Susie dissolved into giggles. Her ham and cheese sandwich sat untouched.

Justin was amused. I wasn't. I had a right to my best friend during our free hour.

I finished my tuna on whole wheat and the chips, then leaned back against a wall to watch the two of them make fools of themselves. Hundreds of birds made the large oaks in the school courtyard their winter home. Kids threw bits of bread on the lawn and the yellow-eyed blackbirds gobbled up the handouts. I hoped a shiny grackle would swoop down and splatter on Carlos' fries.

Justin had cleaned his plate and finished off his French fries. He pointed to one of the guava pastries on his tray. "Do you want it?"

I must have had an incredulous look in my eyes, because he quickly added, "I'm stuffed."

"No, thanks."

"I'll take it." Carlos slipped it off his tray, with the swiftness of a magician.

Susie thought this was quite a trick. She bubbled with laughter.

I shoved back my end of the bench, losing patience. "I gotta go!"

Justin's words sputtered through clenched teeth. "I didn't offer it to you, chum!"

Chapter 3

I carried my English textbook in my leather-trimmed backpack to Mrs. Maxwell's house. I could probably spare a few minutes, while we sat in Dr. Stevens waiting room, to read the story we'd been assigned this week. Mrs. Maxwell insisted I go along on her checkup, though I couldn't understand why she'd need me. Her grandson was driving us there. But Mrs. Maxwell had hired me to be available to her and I took the responsibility seriously.

I wore my black pants and the black-and-yellow striped top that I'd bought last week for the basketball game. I hadn't seen Dr. Stevens in years and Mami wanted me to look presentable. But when I stepped out of my house, I knew my choice had been a mistake. My legs roasted in the heat of the sun.

"Hello, dear," Mrs. Maxwell said when she opened the door. I knew you'd be on time. But that grandson of mine..." She shook her head.

"He's not here yet?"

She pursed her lips. "I'll give him another five minutes, then I'll call a cab."

"He'll make it. You'll see."

"You don't know that boy!"

I sat in the Florida room and read while Mrs. Maxwell puttered around in her bedroom. The story didn't hold my attention. Thoughts of the last few days kept flowing through my head.

Susie had gone off-campus for lunch with Carlos a few times. That left me little choice but to sit with Conchi and her friends for company. They were nice, but so bland! And with them, I didn't feel the closeness I needed to share the most intimate details of my day. Susie called me in the evenings with a full account of her day, babbling with enthusiasm. Mostly, she re-lived step by step everything Carlos had said or done for her. I tried to listen patiently. Yet she couldn't find the time to run across the street to The Grill and Spigot for burgers and a glimpse of Zach. And Carlos, much to my annoyance, found his way to our table whenever we ate in the courtyard.

Justin didn't join us. He sat with Al Suárez, Rick García and Corky Damon—the math freaks. Though I'd never noticed Justin earlier in the year, I now ran into him during class changes, several times a day. He nodded a curt "hello" every time. His friendliness didn't go beyond that and I felt ashamed to have been so abrupt with him.

"I called a cab," Mrs. Maxwell said, sitting next to me.

I shut the book, which had rested idly on my lap. "You gave up on him?"

"It's just as well, dear. I have such trouble getting into that sports utility vehicle his parents gave him. I'm beginning to think he didn't deserve it."

"Those are pretty high off the ground." I preferred to discuss the truck rather than her disappointment in her grandson.

"Listen, dear Maggie. When you choose a young man, keep your eyes open. Make sure he's responsible."

I smiled.

"Do you have a boyfriend?"

I couldn't control the nervous bubble of laughter that escaped me. I wasn't used to discussing this subject with adults. "No. But—"

"Oh!" She laughed. "I can see it in your eyes. There's something cooking!"

"There's this boy in one of my classes," I said between nervous chuckles. "I think we like each other."

"You'll have to tell me about it. First love is so exciting!"

A car horn interrupted our chat.

"I think the taxicab's here." Mrs. Maxwell reached for her purse.

"It could be your grandson," I ventured.

But she scoffed and gave me a cynical look that convinced me I was wrong. "Please, go outside and let the driver know I'm coming right behind you."

The cab took a direct route to the South Miami orthopedist's office. After Mrs. Maxwell got her change back from the driver, I offered her my arm. We stepped up the curb and entered the waiting room.

I made myself comfortable in a nubby-fabric chair, but no sooner had I opened my book than the nurse called in Mrs. Maxwell.

"We're going to take your picture," the blond nurse said. "Dr. Stevens wants another X-ray to check the progress of your leg."

Mrs. Maxwell went to the door then turned and, seeing I hadn't moved from my chair, wiggled her hand with an upward motion. "Up, up! I have a feeling Dr. Stevens would like to see you too."

"Me?"

"I'm sure he'd like to see how well we're getting along."

"Are you sure you want me in there? Isn't he going to examine you?"

"No reason to be shy. It's just my leg. I won't have to undress." Mrs. Maxwell had guessed the source of my concern and conquered my reluctance.

I followed through a maze of doors ending up at the room set up with X-ray equipment. I held Mrs. Maxwell's hand as she sat on the cushioned table and then stretched out on her back.

"Should I straighten the hem of your dress?" I asked.

Mrs. Maxwell grinned and winked. "Quick, before Dr. Stevens walks by and gets an eyeful!"

The nurse positioned Mrs. Maxwell's leg under the intimidating equipment. She motioned me to step outside the room with her. With a click and a hum the film was exposed. When we stepped back in, she took out the cartridge of film and inserted a fresh one in the machine. This time the nurse wanted a side view of the bone. She asked Mrs. Maxwell to lie on her side and bend her healthy leg out of the way.

"I bet I look as graceful as a dead flamingo!" Mrs. Maxwell exclaimed.

The young nurse and I laughed. I didn't have the heart to tell her she was right.

We were ushered into a small examination room, its walls covered with colorful posters of muscles, bones and joints. I was fascinated. But I wondered if a weak-stomached patient with a fresh injury could stand the sight of them. Under the window stood a cushioned table lined with a fresh length of paper from a roll. The paper crackled as Mrs. Maxwell sat on it. I took the only armchair.

Before long, Dr. Stevens and a new nurse entered the room. His brown hair was speckled with gray. Under his starched lab coat, he wore a blue dress shirt and a blue silk tie with realistic rainforest frogs in shades of topaz and jade. I had a hard time taking my eyes off it.

"Everything's looking good," he said. He carried the large sheets of black film under one arm and gripped Mrs. Maxwell's hand. "Is the leg feeling all right?"

The nurse took the X-rays from him and secured them on the reading lamp.

"Can't complain," Mrs. Maxwell answered.

Dr. Stevens' eyes fell on me and a flash of recognition brightened his face. "Maggie Castillo! My goodness! Let me get a look at you."

He offered me his hand, but when I took it, he placed his other hand on my elbow and invited me to stand. "You've turned into a beautiful young woman!"

The faces of the three people in the room with me beamed. I wasn't used to the attention.

"Do you realize I've known Maggie since she was a baby?" he asked no one in particular. "Better than that," he corrected. "I knew her mom and dad for years before she was born. Frank and I went through med school together. We used to meet at a Cuban restaurant on Eight Street for midnight sandwiches and to compare notes before tests. He didn't have much time for me after

30

he met Lucy. But I can't say that I blame him. Did you know I was an usher at their wedding?"

I smiled. "Yes, I've heard."

A puzzled look came over Mrs. Maxwell's face. "I didn't realize your father was a doctor. The love of medicine must run in your blood."

"I guess so," I managed to say.

"Lucy tells me you want to be a nurse," Dr. Stevens said. I knew Mami saw him regularly on the pediatrics floor. "Have you decided what college you'll attend?"

I shrugged my shoulders. "It's kind of early. I'm only a sophomore. But I'll probably stay close to home."

"I'm glad things worked out for you and Mrs. Maxwell. If you can keep her out of trouble, I'll give you a great recommendation for college." His comment got a laugh from Mrs. Maxwell.

She turned to me. "What kind of specialty does your father practice?"

A shadow of sadness floated over the doctor's eyes, but I was used to the question. "He died a long time ago."

"I'm so sorry to hear that," Mrs. Maxwell said softly.

"It's all right. I was only three, I don't really remember him."

"Frank had leukemia," Dr. Stevens explained. "He was still an intern at the hospital. He hadn't started his own practice. His loss was a loss to the field of medicine as well as to his friends." He signaled me closer and pointed to the distinct bone shapes on the film. "See this dark hairline across the tibia? This is the first X-ray of the fracture, three months ago. You can tell from today's picture," he pointed to a second sheet of film with the dull end of his pen, "there is new bone material closing up the gap."

"Wow, that's amazing!" I had always thought of bone as a hard, lifeless material. It was great to see how the living tissue was growing and healing the break.

He pulled up a stool on wheels and sat at Mrs. Maxwell's feet. His hands massaged the place where the fracture had been. "Any pain?"

"Not at all," Mrs. Maxwell answered.

"How about when you put weight on it?"

She scrunched her lips and eyebrows and shook her head. The dimple on her chin was vaguely familiar.

"Good! Then, I'll check it again in three months." With that, he stood up and held Mrs. Maxwell's hand to help her to her feet.

"Frank would be proud of you," Dr. Stevens said. His hand was warm in mine.

"He'd have much reason to be proud," Mrs. Maxwell added.

He pointed a finger at me and cautioned me with a wide grin, "You'd better keep this lady off the tennis courts!"

"I appreciate your keeping me company for my appointment, Maggie," Mrs. Maxwell said at her front door as the taxicab drove away.

"Oh, it was nothing."

She opened the door and dropped her keys into her purse. "There's no reason for you to stay, but if you'd like a soda . . ."

"I'd love one. I think the plants are thirsty too. I want to baby that angel-wing begonia and make sure it keeps its blooms."

"It is a lovely plant."

"I should go home after that, though. I have some reading to do."

"Nothing's more important than that. Make sure you make time for your studies. And for that boy you're fond of," she added with a perky wink, which awakened a rush of shyness in me.

I buried the tip of my finger in the soil at the base of the begonia. The soil didn't feel cool to the touch, as it should when there's moisture in the spongy mixture. When I pulled it out, my finger was powdered with dry dust. It was time to water.

"Here's your soda, dear," Mrs. Maxwell said, leaving behind a cup with ice and a can of Sprite on the table by the wicker sofa.

"Thank you," I said, busy with the outdoor faucet.

"I'm going to change into something more comfortable," she told me, as she left the room. "Help yourself if you'd like anything else. You know where I keep the goodies."

I emptied the first watering can, plucking any brown leaves off the potted plants. I was proud to see them return to health under my care.

The screen door snapped closed behind me, when I returned for a refill. I watched the water reach the full line and bent down, my behind sticking up, to lift the can.

"Nice butt!" a voice behind me said.

I jumped in the air and screamed. "Eek!"

Zach laughed.

My knees went weak at the sight of him and a blaze of heat traveled to my face when I realized he'd gotten such a full view of my rear end. "Whew! What are you doing here?"

"Maggie!" His blue eyes widened in recognition. "Are you the girl who works for Grams?"

"The one and only!" I could never understand why I used stupid phrases only in Zach's presence. It's as if my tongue was out to sabotage me.

"What happened?" Mrs. Maxwell's voice, touched with anxiety, called from her bedroom window. "Was that you screaming, Maggie?"

"It's all right, Grams! I came up behind her and spooked her. I'm ready to take you to the doctor," he shouted, then turned to me and whispered, "You took care of that already, didn't you?"

I nodded.

He pretended to wipe the sweat from his forehead. "Thanks! I'm glad you spared me the trip."

"Zachary! What do you mean showing up at this hour! My appointment with Dr. Stevens was for three-thirty and it's almost five o'clock."

"I'm sorry, Grams! I was practicing." He flashed me a grin full of perfect teeth. I didn't mind his sweaty matted hair or the wet half-moons around the armholes of his sleeveless jersey.

"I thought Mom said you didn't have practice today."

"I came straight from the courts," he yelled in the direction of her window and winked a baby blue at me. Then he brought a finger up to his lips and confided, "I got caught up in a game of pick-up at the park."

Though my heart softened under his close gaze, I felt somewhat disloyal to Mrs. Maxwell. "I'd better water the plants out front."

"Yeah," he said, distracted. "I gotta have something to drink."

When I returned to the Florida room, Mrs. Maxwell was sitting on the wicker chair and Zach paced restlessly by her side. The ice in the glass Mrs. Maxwell had left for me was water. Zach tilted the can of Sprite into his mouth and took a drink.

"I should have guessed you know each other from school."

"Sure, Maggie's in my German class."

My heart pounded with fear. I tried to think back to what I'd said to Mrs. Maxwell earlier. I prayed I hadn't revealed that the boy I liked was in my German class.

"She helps me out with German. She's saved my butt a few times." There was teasing laughter in Zach's eyes as he let out a confident chuckle. Too shook up to hold eye contact, I responded with a dumb bubbly giggle.

"You're lucky to have her around! Though I think you'd learn a better lesson if you were left to flounder on your own." Mrs. Maxwell shook her head. "Do you take any other classes together?"

Zach and I looked at each other. "No," we chorused.

"We have different friends too, Grams," he added. "She hangs around with the Cuban crowd. Always talking in Spanish. Yackity, yak! Yackity yak." He pinched his fingers together in my face as if making quacking shadow-ducks on a wall.

A knot of insecurity twisted in my gut. Did he resent hearing conversation he could not understand? But his gleaming smile dismissed my concerns. Then, with a tilt of his head and a loud slurp, Zach emptied the last of the Sprite.

I guess I must have appeared parched, because he caught me staring as he crushed the empty can with one hand and said, "Uh-oh! Was this your drink?"

"Zachary! Really!"

Mrs. Maxwell made a motion to stand but he waved her back. "Don't bother, Grams. I'll get her another drink."

"It's all right. I can get it myself," I said shyly. I was sorry to have gotten him in trouble. He had made plenty for himself, as it was.

"I'm dying for another one anyway," Zach said, loping to the kitchen in a few quick strides.

Though my heart pounded like a conga drum in his presence, I wanted to dash out of the house. I was flustered and fearful Mrs. Maxwell would reveal my love secret. I gathered up my backpack and said my good-byes as soon as he handed me a cold can of Coke.

"That was the last of the Sprite. You don't mind, do you?"

"The least you can do is give her a ride home, young man."

"You don't have to. I live right around the corner." Though I sounded uninterested, the prospect of riding in his Blazer turned my skin into hen flesh, warm and bumpy.

"It's no problem. I'm going home anyway."

Yes! Zach was giving me a ride home!

He leaned over the older woman and planted a kiss on her head. "Bye, Grams. Sorry I didn't make it on time."

"Come by again, Zachary. See you tomorrow, Maggie."

I made a point of being graceful as I climbed up the high step and into the seat. The car smelled of sweaty sneakers. A smell that up to that moment I had considered foul now magically brought on images of masculinity and strength. His books and papers covered the back seat and a basketball rolled along the back with every turn.

I decided not to open the can of Coke until I got home. The effervescence often caused me to burp. I'd have to transfer out of German class if I let that happen.

"I can't believe you're working for my grandmother." A moist lock of blond hair waggled over his forehead as he turned to me.

"I'm going to study nursing. This job will be great for my resume."

Zach gave me a quizzical smile. "You already know what you're going to major in? Loosen up, Maggie. Give yourself time to enjoy life."

I shrugged, trying to hide the shyness that overpowered me in his presence. "I enjoy what I'm doing. I like taking care of people."

"Whatever!" he said, winking and sending a flash of heat through me.

I directed him to turn right then left. The drive to my house took but a moment. But to me the experience felt like a ride on Aladdin's magic carpet.

"It was good seeing ya!" he said as he drove off. That, too, I memorized.

As I ran to my bedroom to call Susie, I was amazed how true the jasmine's answer had been today.

"You'll never guess what happened!" I blurted as soon as I heard Susie's voice. "I'm still out of breath!"

"¡Chica! I've been trying to reach you." Her voice was light as freshly beaten merengue. "I've got some news of my own."

"I doubt you can top this!" My words came out like popping corn, fast and airy.

"Wait 'til you hear what I've got to tell you!"

"Susie! Give me a chance! I called you!"

"Go ahead, *chica*, you first," she said, laughing.

I paused for drama. "Zach came over to Mrs. Maxwell's!"

"To do what? Cut her lawn or something?"

"She's his grandmother!"

Susie drew a breath. "*¡Mentira!* You're kidding, right?"

"He drove me home!"

She hollered victoriously. I could almost see her elbow pump down and her thumbs-up sign. "You got a ride in the Blazer!"

"Remember I told you Mrs. Maxwell's grandson was driving us to the doctor's office? Would you believe she was talking about Zach?"

"You were with him all afternoon?" Susie sounded incredulous.

"No, he was held up, so we took a cab. But he showed up after."

"And he wanted to take you home? That's a good sign, Maggie," she teased.

"He said he was happy he'd seen me! I'm so glad I wore my new outfit. I could have been wearing some horrendous jogging get-up."

"Lucky!"

"He even got me a Coke. Listen to this." I held the receiver close to the can and pulled on the tab. "Did you hear that precious whoosh? I'm going to drink it slow . . ."

"You ought to save the can. This is historical! And so is what I've got to tell you!"

"Okay, on with your story." I laughed and lay back on the yellow and blue covers of my daybed.

"Carlos asked me out." Her voice was like a little girl's who'd been handed a chunk of sugarcane.

I should have seen it coming, yet the news took me by surprise. "On a date or are you two . . . you know, going together?"

"On a date." She giggled excitedly. "I think the other is coming up."

"Susie, that's wonderful!" I said, though their togetherness unsettled me. "When's he taking you out?"

"Friday night." She paused. Her tone lacked the confidence she'd had until now. "He wants you to come with us."

I laughed. "That's a new one. Carlos wants me to tag along on your date?"

She hesitated. I could tell something was up. "You'd be Justin's date. You remember him, don't you?"

I sat up. "No way!"

"He's cute, Maggie. Really cute!" She dragged out the words as though imploring.

I opened the mini-blinds to let some light in. Somehow the room was closing in on me. But only the orange rays of the setting sun filtered in. "I hardly know the boy."

"That's just it! You'll get to know him better."

I sat at my dressing table and ran the brush through the end of my ponytail. "I can't anyway. This is Thanksgiving weekend."

"So? Are you a turkey? You're sure acting like one, *chica*."

"I wouldn't miss Friday night's game against Miami Park for anything."

"That's where they're taking us, nut head!" Susie insisted. "And we'll go out for dessert later. You won't miss a single play by Zach."

"Susie, I can't take the chance to have Zach see me with another boy. Not the way things are going now."

"He won't be able to spot you in the bleachers. There's gonna be a big crowd." Susie had an answer for everything. "Besides, he'll be too busy playing."

"My heart's not in it." I smacked my brush down on the dresser.

"Maggie." She used the last device left to her, putting an edge of sadness to her voice: "My parents said I couldn't go with Carlos alone. But if you came along on a double date, they'd okay it. You know I'm dying to go out with Carlos."

"So you arranged a date for me?"

"No! ¡Te lo juro! Cross my heart!" Her defensive tone seemed genuine. "It was the boys' idea."

I thought it over for a moment. "Well, what are friends for?"

"I'll be at your mercy forever!" She was floating on clouds of merengue again. "Justin will be calling you any minute!"

"I can't believe you gave him my number!"

She laughed. "He asked for it. I gotta go! See ya!"

Chapter 4

I kept Mami company in the kitchen after setting the Thanksgiving table for two. We had called Abuela in Chicago to wish her a good holiday. When Mami thought I couldn't hear her, she'd given her mother a few suggestions for Christmas presents for me. Mami told Abuela that the jogging shoes I wanted were very expensive, and she didn't want her mother spending what little money she had on us. But Abuela usually came through for me.

The aroma of roast turkey was making my mouth water. The juices from the ground beef and pork stuffing, with raisins, olives and other tasty morsels, were dribbling onto the roasting pan. I couldn't wait for Mami to pronounce the bird ready. "If you're busy with other stuff, I can get going with the carving," I suggested in Spanish, the language we used at home.

Mami raised an eyebrow. "I like my turkey carved, not diced. Thank you."

I laughed, snapping off a chunk of crusty skin and putting it in my mouth.

"The turkey has to rest for twenty minutes after it comes out of the oven."

"I don't know, Mami," I said, eyeing the golden bird closely. "It doesn't look tired to me."

"Here, put the *platanitos* on the table, before I get tired of *you.*"

I straightened out the lace tablecloth, which made its second of three annual appearances on Thanksgiving. We used it first at Easter and lastly on Christmas Eve, for the traditional roast pork Cuban feast.

I doubted Justin would call today. He'd be busy with his family for the holiday. Susie and I wondered if our plans were still on, since I hadn't heard from him. Carlos had urged Justin to make the call and gotten assurances but no results. Susie and Carlos were anxious because of the condition Mr. and Mrs. Domínguez had set over the date. To prevent a change of heart, Susie had assured her parents that everything was all set. She planned to ask them to drive her and me to the gym on Friday if the date fell through. There, Susie and Carlos would team up.

We had never done anything behind our parents' backs before, and I felt uncomfortable about it. I wondered how I'd look them in the eye next time I went over to Susie's house. But I agreed to it, as long as Susie didn't leave my sight the whole evening. This would be an easier task than making conversation with a boy I hardly knew. Besides, it seemed Justin had agreed to the date as a favor to a friend and I was soured on the whole idea.

"*Ven aquí,*" Mami said when I returned to the kitchen. "I have a job for you."

She assigned me the task of mashing the garlic cloves the old fashioned way, with mortar and pestle. Mami didn't like using the food processor to chop garlic. She believed the only way to extract the pungent oil was to bruise the cloves. I watched as she stirred the garlic into the heated olive oil, holding the saucepan over the heat just long enough to soften the mashed cloves. The hot oil sputtered when she poured in the juice of a sour orange, then she drizzled the sizzling *mojo* over tender steaming *yuca*. My nose followed her movements and my stomach gurgled with anticipation. I could no longer resist. With a fork, I stole a morsel of the cooked tuber.

"If you don't carve the turkey now, I'll finish off the *yuca* before you can set it on the table!" I threatened her, laughing.

Mami tossed me a self-assured glance. "I outdid myself again! *¿Verdad?* Don't you think?"

"I can't wait! I'll put the beans and rice on the table while you carve." I was starving. She needed a push.

I was glad to see her pick up the sharpened knife and make the first cut. The juices dribbled out of the sliced crunchy skin. "I'm glad I got the day off," Mami said.

"Yeah, me too."

"Your papi and I celebrated our first Thanksgiving in Miami. We didn't have this holiday in Cuba, you know." The knife and fork were motionless in her hands for a moment. "It's very meaningful to me now."

"I know." I'd heard it before, every Thanksgiving. "You thank God for everything He's given us. And you thank Him for what He hasn't given us, because He knows what's best for us."

Mami laughed. "It may sound funny, but it's true."

"I don't know how you can thank Him for taking Papi from you so early."

Mami nodded, a faint smile lingering on her lips. "I think Papi went straight to Heaven. If he'd lived longer, knowing your father, they might have closed the pearly gates on him."

"If that makes you feel better . . ." I found it hard to understand how he'd been taken from her, the man in the photograph on her nightstand, the father I loved but never got to know. Mami had dated several men during my childhood, but none had been suitable in the end. I was worried she'd spend the rest of her life alone.

"Anyway, there's many other things for which to be thankful," she said. "We have good health. We have a nice home. I have a job . . ."

"*We* have jobs!"

"That's right!" Mami held a sliver of white meat between her fingers for me.

I bit it off. "Uhm! *¡Qué rico!* Delicious!" I said with my mouth full.

"What's Mrs. Maxwell doing today?"

"She went to her daughter's for dinner." A picture of Zach flashed into my mind. I saw his freckled face scrunching with effort as he carved their roast turkey. "I told her I'd take her a plate tomorrow, so she can have a taste of our Cuban dishes. Is that okay?"

"Of course!" Mami said. "That's why I turned down Lydia's offer to join them for dinner. I love having leftovers."

"Do we really have to go to their house for dessert tonight?" Lydia was Mami's childhood friend from Cuba. They considered us family, and that was part of the problem. Lydia and Rafael's house would be filled with old relatives whom I saw once a year and whose prolonged absences I never missed. Every new arrival would demand the traditional hugs and kisses. I'd spend the first half of the evening wiping lipstick and moist smacks off my cheeks and the second half taking everyone tiny cups of Cuban coffee. The house would reverberate with shotgun blasts of conversation and laughter and there would be nothing of interest for someone my age. Their children were grown and out of the house.

Mami's answer was delivered with a meaningful look. "You might just have a good time."

"Oh, no!" I realized something suddenly: "If you got Thanksgiving off, does that mean you have to work on Christmas?"

Mami gave me a little pout. "I'm sorry. That's the way these things go. We'll be able to spend Christmas Eve together."

"We're talking about Christmas day, Mami! A day to be with family!"

"I know, *mi vida*. But the hospital must keep running and the patients still need nursing, even on Christmas." I hated the apologetic look on her face. It didn't bring me any comfort. "I talked to Lydia about it. They're expecting you for the day."

"You didn't?"

I remembered a holiday at Lydia's house a couple of years back, when Mami could not trade her shift. Her friend Marge didn't mind working for her on Christmas because she was Jewish, and Mami often covered for Marge on Rosh Hashanah and Yom Kippur. But that Christmas, Marge and her family left on vacation. So I was banished to Lydia's. Mami allowed me to take only a board game from among the gifts she'd given me. After the guests left, Rafael assumed the duty of amusing me by playing it with me. We set up the game on the rickety table on their back porch, the only place Lydia allowed him to chomp on his smelly cigars, and we played it over and over. When I went home, I hid the game in the attic, to make sure I would never again be put through such misery.

"I can't leave you alone on Christmas," she said.

"I'll go to Susie's. Her parents won't mind."

"Yes they will. It puts them on the spot. They'll feel they'd have to buy you a present."

"I'll tell them not to worry about a gift for me."

"Lydia and Rafael are looking forward to sharing Christmas with you," she said, as though she hadn't heard me. "And they're looking forward to seeing us tonight too. There's nothing else going on for you. You'll have the rest of the weekend to do as you please. Have you made any plans?"

I shrugged. "Susie wants us to double-date to the game Friday night. She fixed me up with a new boy in school."

"That sounds like fun!"

"Well, if he doesn't call me up soon and ask me himself, I'm not going."

"Don't be so arrogant. He's probably working up the courage to call you. Boys have a hard time asking girls out, you know."

"You're always telling me to have self-respect, but you side with a stranger on this one."

"It's one thing to have self-respect, Maggie, and another to be haughty." She looked directly into my eyes. "You and Susie stick together all evening. That way you'll *keep* your self-respect."

When we returned home from Lydia's house, I poured myself a glass of soda. I set the glass on the wicker trunk in my bedroom and listened to my phone messages before I powered the volume for MTV.

There was a call from Susie. Hardly a surprise, since it seemed she was calling me hourly now that we were down to the wire. I figured the next message would be from her too.

"Hey, Maggie?" said a male voice. I jerked around and stared at the answering machine. The motion made my glass of iced soda teeter on the edge of the trunk. I grabbed it just in time.

"It's me, Justin-from-school." (He put the words together as though the second part was his last name.) "Carlos says you're waiting for a phone call from me. I guess you're not home. I should have known. It's Thanksgiving and all. You're probably somewhere for dinner." There was a pause. He seemed to be looking for the right words. "We'll pick you up around six thirty tomorrow. We're going to the game and we'll get something to eat later. Bye."

I clicked off the Cranberries in the middle of their silent act, rewound the answering machine tape and listened to his message again.

I was furious! He hadn't even given me a chance to say yes or no! I dialed Susie's number and she picked up the phone on the first ring.

"Justin left a message for me. He says he'll be at my house by six-thirty."

"Great!" Susie exclaimed. "What a relief!"

"This isn't starting out so well. He's full of himself!" I said. "He's taking it for granted that I've agreed to go!"

"¡Ay, chica! You wouldn't have turned him down anyway. I was counting on you. I'll owe you forever."

47

She had a way of soothing me out of a bad mood. My brain was scheming a way she could pay back. "I would have liked the courtesy of waiting for my answer."

Susie laughed. "I'm sure Carlos told him we were all set. Besides, what do you expect when he's leaving a message on a machine?" Susie sounded like a mother. "We'll have a great time. You'll see."

"You'll have a great time. But, guess what! It's pay-off time!"

"Already? We haven't even gone out with the guys yet."

"Well, look at this one as a Thanksgiving good deed." I took a short swallow. I'd be going against Mami's advice by asking. "Mami has to work on Christmas and I don't have a place to go. Well, I do. She made plans for me, but her friends don't have any kids and it's so boring there."

"Super! You can sleep over Christmas Eve and spend the day with us."

I held back my relief. "Are you sure it'd be okay with your parents?"

"Of course! I guess . . ."

"They don't have to get me a present or anything. It's not right to invite myself and expect they'd, you know—"

"I'm gonna get something for you anyway. Just like we did last year, remember."

Susie and I had exchanged Christmas presents. Neither one of us had worked last year, so it was really our parents' money we had spent. This year, we had our own paychecks. I'd remind Mami. I was sure she wouldn't mind my new plans.

~~~

Justin wore dark gray pants and a dressy T-shirt with wide gray and blue stripes. He'd tucked the shirt loosely into the belt line of the pants, letting the small red logo at its base show.

"Are you all set?" His eyes looked steely gray in the shadows of our front porch.

"We're off, Mami!" I yelled, plucking a jasmine from the vine for good luck.

"Have fun! And get home at a decent hour," Mami said from the kitchen.

"Your hair looks nice. I like it when you wear it down," Justin said, as we made our way to the car.

Self-consciously, I flung a long strand over my shoulder. I was relieved to see Susie and Carlos in the back seat of the Honda. Susie had curled the wispy ends of her hair around her face and colored her lips an earthy rose.

"I thought you'd be driving, Carlos," I said.

Justin shut the car door on my side as I settled into the front seat.

"Nah. I like Justin's car better." The grin on his face was unconvincing. I had a feeling he'd worked it out this way so he could free up his hands. I shuddered, but was relieved my date would have to concentrate on the road.

Justin headed back to the main road and pushed in a tape. "Do you like rhythm and blues?"

"Sure," I shrugged.

The boys began to discuss predictions for our school game. I stole a glance at Susie.

She mouthed a silent "thanks" and beamed at me.

When we arrived, the school gym was filling up with a noisy crowd. There were still enough seats to make a selection. I headed our group, while Justin gently prodded me with his hand on my elbow. The possessive familiarity of it irritated me. But when I saw Carlos leading Susie by the hand, like a goat on a rope, I was grateful for my fortune.

"This row looks good. Don't you think?" I asked Justin.

He turned to Carlos. "Do you like these seats?"

"I don't want to sit five rows behind home bench." Carlos continued up a few more steps followed by a faithful Susie. "Let's move up to the top."

I had come to keep my eyes on Zach. I didn't want to sit way up in the clouds, where I couldn't distinguish his face from the others. "We'll get a good view of the players from here," I said.

"We'll be able to see the whole court from higher up," Carlos insisted, his dark brows gathering close. "We'll catch every play."

Justin's gaze went from Carlos to me.

"Look," I whispered to him, so Susie wouldn't give me away. "My eyesight is not very good from a distance."

Justin turned to Carlos. "We're going to take these seats. We'll meet you after the game."

"I want to be close to Maggie," I heard Susie say.

"All right," Carlos' reluctant tone reached me. "We'll sit a few rows behind them."

When I spotted Zach, in his regulation yellow jersey and royal blue boxers, a thrill ran through me. The number nine, his team number, had taken on a special significance in my world. Whenever I encountered it on billboards, addresses, price tags, a picture of his face zipped into focus in my mind. Though he was a sophomore, Zach played forward on the Glades Ridge varsity team. During intramural games the year before, he had shown potential, and so when three senior players graduated, Coach

Dunhill had tapped Zach for a vacant spot on the varsity team. As I watched Zach run down the court, warming up with his teammates and passing the ball to each other, I knew that all my discomfort of this evening would be worth it.

"Where's your glasses?" Justin asked.

"I don't wear any," I told him, without taking my eyes off the court.

"You ought to have your eyes checked, then."

"It's not too bad from here. Really."

Both teams gathered in the center of the court and, with a starting whistle, the referee tossed the ball in the air for the opening jump. The centers leaped and the ball was tapped into Zach's hands. He took off, dribbling into his court, the opposing forward trailing him. Zach's blond hair sparkled. For a moment, he had a clear path to the basket. He took it, and his two-handed lay-up shot gave us the first score of the game. The home crowd rose and cheered.

I stole a glance at Susie, wanting to share my pride in Zach, but she didn't look my way. She and Carlos waved their hands over their heads and joined the noisy fans. Justin raised a victory fist, and a trail of goose pimples crawled up my arm as it accidentally rubbed against his.

The ball was put into play again. The ten players worked their way up and down the court, scoring at each end and restarting from behind the line after every basket. The rubber-sole squeaks of the players' sneakers on the shiny wood floor carried over the noise of the crowd. I kept my eyes glued on Zach throughout the action and even during time-outs. His cheeks reddened and his forehead glistened with sweat. He was a strong player. My breath fluttered with pride. Both teams scored consistently during the first half. Fortunately, our team kept up at least an eight point margin.

When the action stopped during halftime, Justin offered to buy me a Coke.

"Want to come along?"

"Sure, I need to stretch my legs," I said. The players had run into the locker room and I wouldn't miss out seeing Zach while I was gone. Besides, Glades Ridge cheerleaders were going to perform a routine on the court and I didn't care for their silly moves and calls. None of my friends were on the squad.

"You're really into the game!"

I shrugged. I couldn't tell Justin what my real interest on the court was. "I'd be upset if Miami Park beat us."

I worried about the long line at the concession stand. But we were served with time enough to return to our seats.

In the fourth quarter, with Glades Ridge leading by only four points, the Miami Park forward guarding Zach blocked him. Zach dribbled down the court and was getting ready to shoot when the player's arm and shoulder made contact with him. He was allowed a free throw. Zach concentrated, bouncing the ball at his feet a couple of times. His wrists and fingertips followed through the release of the ball. His shot landed on the hoop and the ball rolled on it, like a toy train on a circular track. The crowd sat on the edge of their seats. The ball completed a circle and rimmed out. Zach's hands clenched at his sides for a moment.

"Damn! That should've been an easy shot," Justin said.

My eyes turned to him. I took a deep breath. I was afraid he'd read my feelings for Zach if I said something in his defense.

When Glades Ridge got possession of the ball again, Zach received a pass and took off with the ball. Miami Park's forward kept up with him, running alongside. Suddenly, Zach changed direction and charged into him. He rammed his opponent. The Miami Park player fell heavily to the ground as Zach dribbled past. A whistle rang out and a technical foul was called against Zach.

"He blew it!" Justin said. "The guy's gonna screw up the game for everyone. He's got to keep his anger in check."

"I suppose you're good in that department?" I asked.

Justin's eyes dug into me. "I'm working on it. But at least I'm no prima donna."

Coach Dunhill called in a substitute to replace Zach. On his way to the bench behind the sideline, Zach gazed up at the crowd. Thinking I'd caught his eye, I waved at him, concealing my hand from Justin. But Zach turned and sat to watch Miami Park shoot for the point, his blue "9" glowing at the Glades Ridge crowd.

The player took his time preparing, then shot the ball. The backboard drummed. The ball bounced off it and fell straight through the net, earning him a point and another free throw.

Zach got up. I figured the anxiety was getting to him. Miami Park was inching closer to a tied score. The player took careful aim, then released the ball with an extension of his slightly flexed knees. The ball flew cleanly through the hoop. The Miami Park fans rose and screamed with joy.

Zach turned away from the court. He didn't look happy. But I had little time to dwell on that. Kelly Rogers, in her tiny cheerleading skirt, ran to him with a towel and a cup of water. He drank from it, little streams of water dripping from the sides, while the girl reached up and wiped the sweat from his brow. To my amazement, she put her arms around his neck, tipping up on her toes to circle him. I was livid! While still in her grasp, Zach took another gulp, tilting his head back and facing the crowd.

I saw my chance. Without a moment to consider my actions, I put my arm behind Justin and shoved his head against mine. With our cheeks pressed together, I glanced at Zach. I could swear we made eye contact. I was satisfied.

Justin's cheek was warm and smooth, and his neck gave off a spicy, lemony scent. When I let go of him, he stared at me with a mixture of disbelief and empathy. I thought I detected a pink flush to his ears. *Good going, Maggie!* I chided myself. *Now you've given him false expectations.*

Justin took his hand in mine and squeezed it. "It's okay . . . We still have a chance to win."

I had no choice but to let him hold my hand the rest of the game. I wished I'd brought a box of raisins or M&Ms—or anything that required two hands to eat: one hand to hold the box and the other to bring the treat to your mouth. This was a technique that Elena García, an experienced upperclassman, had shared with us to keep a boy at bay. In a serious pinch, a girl could make a bag of M&Ms last through an entire date by slowly measuring them out one at a time.

Glades Ridge didn't hold its lead. What's more, Miami Park scored two more baskets and won the close game in the final seconds.

My hand felt clammy when Justin finally released it.

We joined Susie and Carlos on the court and headed out to the parking lot. It's a good thing Carlos was leading her by the hand or she might have tripped and fallen on the gravel path: She didn't take her dreamy eyes off his face while he talked. To my dismay, Justin took a possessive hold of my hand again.

My palm felt moist and stiff. It was a relief when I worked it free and beat him to the handle of the car door.

Susie, Justin and I ordered chicken and beef tacos at Pepe's Cantina, a Mexican restaurant popular among teens with tall appetites yet short on cash. Carlos wanted beef fajitas, which came with infinite rights to steamy flour tortilla refills. He also ordered tomato soup with cheese and avocado chunks floating in it. The young waiter leafed through the menu searching for the dish.

"You won't find it in there. Just bring me the soup and sides of cheese and avocados. I'll put it together."

The white-shirted waiter raised a brow and left without a word. Susie and I made noises of disgust.

"Don't knock it! This is what I have for breakfast every morning."

Susie slid down in the booth bench, faking a fainting spell. "For breakfast?" she asked weakly.

Carlos was enjoying the effect his unique habit had worked on us.

"I crush Ritz crackers in it when there's no avocados."

"Whatever happened to a man-size batch of scrambled eggs and bacon?" Justin asked, ganging up with the girls and laughing.

"Or a sweet *café con leche* and toasted Cuban bread?" By the time I shuffled like a zombie into the kitchen in the mornings,

Mami was gone to work. So I fixed my own warm milk with a touch of the thick and powerful Cuban coffee Mami brewed every morning and I toasted and buttered my own crusty bread, to dip in the cup.

"Nothing beats my soup!" Carlos scoffed.

His dish was served first. The waiter took his time wiping a clean table and eyeing Carlos in the process of dicing his avocado slices and sprinkling shredded cheese in the thick red liquid. With each spoonful, the melting cheese stretched from the bowl to his mouth, forming a thin, sagging bridge.

"Let me give you a hand." Susie threatened to wind the thread of cheese around her pointed finger.

Carlos leaned away from her, the attached cheese stretching thinly.

Justin scissored it with his knife and mine.

"Cut it out!"

"You mean cut it off!" Justin teased, sliding one blade against the other, as if sharpening a barber's razor.

But when the cheese filament broke off, snapped back into the soup and splashed red dots onto his yellow golf shirt, Carlos ceased smiling. His dark brows twisted with annoyance. Susie dipped a paper napkin in her glass of water and attempted to wipe the stains. She succeeded only in smearing the dots into a brick-colored patch across the front of his shirt. I knew to lay off the guy after that. I guessed Justin felt the same way, because he brought up a new subject.

"That forward isn't doing much for Glades Ridge. He should be shipped back to junior varsity, 'til his head cools off."

"Sherwood?" Carlos asked. "Yeah, he loses it once in a while."

"He pulls his weight," I snapped. I wanted to chip away at Carlos' and Justin's egos. "You're too new to Glades Ridge. You don't know what our players are made of."

Justin gave me a cocky smile. "From tonight's game, I'd say melted mozzarella."

Carlos let out a jeering howl.

Susie gave him an angelic smile, quickly replaced by a smirk of guilt when I pinned my gaze on her.

"I didn't see either one of you on the court tonight!" I snapped.

"Geez, Mag! The guy's a jerk. I can't believe you're defending him."

"You don't even know him, Carlos. Don't judge people unless you do."

"And you do?" Carlos' brows shot up in that disdainful expression of his that had the power to set my blood to a steaming boil.

"They're friends, sort of," Susie said meekly, prompted by my stern look.

"Well, Mag. As *guajiros* are known to say: *Dime con quien andas, y te diré quien eres.*"

"Hey! English, man!"

Rigid in my seat, I ignored Justin and instead seared Carlos with a stare. "Meaning?"

"So you're a *gringa* now? Can't understand Spanish?"

Susie, lids lowered, whispered, "There's a *gringo* among us, Carlos."

"Justin's not a *gringo*. Just's good people."

"I know exactly how the saying goes, Carlos." I leaned forward into his face. "I'm not sure how you're applying it."

"So, clue me in!" Justin demanded.

"It's an old Spanish proverb." Susie's eyes darted nervously from Carlos to Justin. "It goes: *Tell me who you hang around with, and I'll tell you who you are.*"

Carlos shoved his empty plate to the middle of the table as if staking out his territory in our war of words. "I'll bet you want to join Sherwood's crowd across the street for burgers."

"I never said that." I stole an anxious glance at Susie. "But what if I wanted to?"

Carlos' thick brows rose. "The hangout of the Ill and Bigots?"

"The Grill and Spigot," Susie explained to Justin.

"I'm not dense." Justin crumpled a napkin into a tight ball.

My eyes squinted with rage. "Are you suggesting Zach's prejudiced?"

"I'm telling you your precious friend hates Cubans."

My insides swirled with fear. If Carlos were right, would Zach be able to open his heart to me? Anger and insecurity were turning my world into a muddled mess. It couldn't be true. Zach had been friendly and natural with me. "You seem to have a bad habit of determining people's character without getting to know them. *That*, Carlos, is called prejudice. When you meet the guy and spend some time with him, let's have this talk again."

"I don't need to meet him to know his reputation."

"Now who's the bigot?"

"Look, Margarita, I have plenty of American friends. I hang around with Corky and Justin and a bunch of others. I'm not the kind to waste my time with people who don't care about me."

"Okay. That's enough. You guys aren't gonna to change each other's minds," Justin broke in, to my relief. "Let's get outta here!"

Susie filled the awkward silence with light chatter while we waited for the check. I couldn't keep my mind on her words because so many disturbing thoughts danced in my head. At the same time I was concerned about paying for my own bill. I would insist on taking care of my meal. If Justin paid, he'd feel entitled him to a feel-up, or who knew what else. It was bad enough that I would have to kiss him good night at the door.

But when the bill arrived, Justin wouldn't even let me peek at it. He and Carlos divided the cost between them. I dug out a ten and pushed it at him.

"Put that away," Justin said. "You're my date."

Susie gave me a sly wink, and Justin peeled a mint from a roll he'd bought at the register and handed it to me.

"Thanks," I said. A cold trickle of apprehension ran down my spine. I was trapped.

We got back in the Honda and Justin turned south on Red Road.

"Where are we going?" I looked straight at him and pointed my thumb at the rear window. "My house is that way."

Chapter 5

Carlos laughed. "What are you doing sitting way over there, Sus?"

Obediently, Susie slid over to the center seat and adjusted her seat belt. Carlos had his arm around her before it clicked in place, and he drew her to him before I could turn back to face the front again.

"You didn't answer my question," I persisted, giving Justin a fiery side glance.

"We'll just go for a drive. I want to show you my old school."

"In the middle of the night?"

"There's a nice place to park on the grounds." His smile appeared harmless. "It's right by the bay."

"We're not going to see anything in pitch darkness. What's your plan? To aim your high beams on the building?" He had little interest in showing me the architectural features of Masterson's Academy, I was sure. But I was too embarrassed to object. I knew if we took a vote on our destination, I'd be outnumbered three to one.

Justin gave a slight toss of his chin. "I keep a flashlight in the glove compartment. Check and see if it works."

The glove compartment light came on and I hoped he wouldn't notice how flustered I was. The sounds of kissing and heavy breathing could be heard now over the stereo. My anger at Carlos was spilling over to Susie. I had to fight to tolerate my best friend's feelings for the guy who'd gotten me so worked up. I took the red flashlight out and tested it to make myself busy. The light wobbled in my hand and the beam fell on Justin's face.

He scrunched his brow and blinked his eyes. "Whoa! You're blinding me!"

"I'm sorry!" I said, giggling nervously.

Justin turned off the headlights, then veered off the paved road into an empty lot. In the darkness, the limestone gravel crunching under the weight of the wheels seemed to glow. A tall chain-link fence surrounded the adjacent property. A handful of spotlights bathed the enclosed grounds with a soft light. But it didn't reach beyond the fence. I shivered with apprehension. The only light for our use was that which reflected from the white rock on the ground.

"Here it is. This is Masterson's," Justin said, turning off the engine. "We're in the student parking lot."

I could barely make out the outline of a two-story building and several other smaller structures within the enclosure. Trees and hedges by the main building cut off much of the view. It was as if only the rich who could afford Masterson's steep tuition were privileged to set eyes on the grounds. I'd heard that the college prep school expected high academic effort from students. I wondered what had caused Justin to transfer out.

"Do you miss it?"

He looked the building over. "Hell, no!"

The passionate necking in the back seat was steaming up the car windows and making my skin crawl.

"Not even your friends?"

"Ooh! You're hurting my ribs with your elbow!" Susie cried out.

"I'm sorry." The soothing quality in Carlos' voice worked the opposite effect on me. "Is that better?"

"Uh huh," said Susie.

"They weren't really my friends." Justin's eyebrows gathered together for a moment. "You find out when things get rough."

"What happened? Why did you leave?"

Justin took his time answering. "It's a long story."

"Don't tell it here, please!" Carlos piped up angrily. "Go for a walk—and take your time telling her all about it."

"Come on," Justin said, opening his door. "There's something I want to show you anyway."

I opened my door and jumped out. A sense of duty told me to stay by Susie's side and keep her in line. But, cooped up in the car, the implied expectation that Justin and I should carry on like the two in the back had tied a knot in my stomach. Despite the darkness and isolation of the place, I breathed easier again. I filled my lungs. The air tasted salty and moist.

"Are you going to use the flashlight or just hold it?"

I gave Justin a nervous chuckle. "I'd forgotten it was still in my hand." I aimed the stream of light at the two-story building.

"That's the main school building," Justin said. "It's where most of the classes meet. The next building over is the central hall. It's used for lunch and assemblies. You can see the gym on the other side of it."

I swayed the flashlight in my hand, painting the large structures with streaks of light. "Which one's the gym?" I asked.

Justin's hand wrapped around my wrist. I was very aware of the warmth of his touch. He aimed the light higher up. "There, the one with the barrel tile roof." Then, with a slight turn of his wrist, the light fell on two smaller buildings dotting the grounds. "The science teachers get the portable classrooms way in the back. I think they're afraid someone will set off an explosion one day, so they keep the labs in disposable buildings."

The pleasant sound of his laughter caused me to smile.

"Come on," he said, taking the flashlight from my hand and winding his fingers with mine. "This isn't what I wanted to show you."

As we worked our way over the rough stones to the back of the property, the gentle murmur of ocean waves helped soothe my anxiety over the fix I was in. I wasn't sure where Justin was leading. I wasn't sure I wanted to follow. The tide was out. The line of washed-up seaweed lay several feet out of the reach of the gently lapping waters. A soft breeze caressed my hair. Justin bathed the edge of the rocky shore with light, and hundreds of tiny crabs waved yellow claws, as if in a synchronized salute. When the beam of light zig-zagged over them a second time, the silent creatures scurried out of sight. Justin and I shared a soft laugh, and needles and pins tingled my neck when his eyes met mine.

Justin pointed the light to a wooden pier, which extended fifty feet or so into the water on the fenced side of the grounds. "Have you ever been on the water at night? Come see how peaceful it is."

"Excuse me?" I said shrilly, as though he needed to be cleared up on this. "There's a fence between us and the dock!"

He chuckled. "So?"

"You don't expect me to climb over it! It must be six feet high!"

"Would I put you through all that work?" His lips fanned out in a wide grin. "See how the fence juts out into the water? At low tide, you can make it around the end."

"You're kidding! Right?"

"Hand me your shoes."

"I'm not wading in this water!"

He looked into my eyes. His crooked half-smile and the amusement in his eyes were disconcerting. "Are you afraid of sea monsters?"

I squared my shoulders. "I take it you've done this before?"

Justin slipped off his loafers and rolled up the cuffs of his pants. "Many times. I'll go first and hold your hand, if it makes you feel better."

My sandals came off and I pulled up my pant legs as high as the tight fabric permitted. Justin waded in and reached for my hand. This time, I was eager to have him hold it. I prayed that the night crawlers and swimmers had scattered at the sound of our voices. The water lapped at my ankles. It was acceptably chilly. The rocky bottom was another matter. My pampered feet weren't used to the jagged rocks. I teetered and wobbled with each painful step. Though Justin was clearly amused, his arm held steady and his grip on my hand firmed up.

"Just a few more steps," he reassured me.

As we rounded the end of the fence, the water sloshed around my calves. My heart pounded in my chest. With my hand gripping Justin's for dear life, we dashed to the shore and I breathed a sigh of relief. I wasn't about to let on how frightening it had been to wade through the dark waters.

"Let's make a run for the dock!" I shouted.

"I'm right behind ya!"

The rocky ground hampered my speed, but I had a feeling the run wasn't as tough for Justin. He was being a sport. He lagged behind me all the way to the end of the wooden dock.

"This is the only thing I miss about Masterson's," said Justin, catching up with me. "No public high school has a private cove."

"This is nice."

He traced the shoreline with a finger. "See the mangroves growing at the edge of the water? Follow them 'til you see a break. That's the entrance to the cove from the bay."

I scanned the dark horizon. "Let me try the flashlight," I suggested.

"You'd be wasting your time. The light won't reach that far." Justin sat, letting his feet dangle from the end of the dock. He set down his shoes and the flashlight on the planks behind him. "Let your eyes get used to the dark. You'll see things you won't otherwise notice."

He patted a place for me by his side and I took it, though I wasn't sure I wanted my feet hovering so close to the watery void. Instead, I crossed my legs pow-wow style.

"Have you found time to run lately?" he asked.

"Not much." I hate breaking the ice with a date I hardly know; we end up discussing the most inane subjects. My mind kept shifting to thoughts of Zach and what it'd be like to be with him instead. "The sun goes down early now. My mom doesn't want me running at night."

"I do some jogging too, mostly around my neighborhood. Sometimes I run in Lowe Grove Park."

"Me too! I haven't been there since I started working, though."

"So, tell me about your job."

"Oh, there's not much to it. I check in on an older lady who's recovering from a broken leg. She's Zach Sherwood's grandmother. You know who he is, don't you?" My heart lurched with pride, having a legitimate reason to bring up his name.

"Nope, I don't think I do."

"Hello!" I said playfully. "He's the forward on our team. Number nine. The one Carlos has it in for."

Justin gave a dismissive shrug. "Yeah, I know who you mean now."

"Anyway, I have to check everyday to see that she's all right and go with her to the doctor. That sort of thing." I could see my mention of Zach hadn't won me any points. "Do you have a job?"

Justin looked up. "Are you kidding? My dad thinks work builds character. If I end up without a job, he finds one for me." He pursed his lips. "He wants me to study engineering and join him in his business."

"What's wrong with that? My dad was a doctor; my mom's a nurse. I'm interested in medicine, too. Besides, you said you're a math whiz." I shot him a teasing smile.

"I didn't say that!" His eyebrows gathered in a frown, but his eyes glinted with amusement. "I said I liked math." He flicked a pebble into the dark water. "I just wish he'd let me make up my own mind. Right now, he's got me copying blacklines at the machine."

"That sounds pretty technical. I'm impressed."

Justin shrugged. "It's just a large machine that copies engineering drawings. It's a pretty clean job. I go in a couple of times a week and catch up on the printing at his office."

"Wow! An indoor job in a professional office . . ."

"He doesn't always make it that easy. I worked on a construction site last summer, at one of his new developments. Summer weather was a pain! When the sun wasn't blistering our backs, the rains drowned us. I think he chose the job as punishment."

"For what?"

He gazed past the opening of the cove. "Never mind."

Behind him, I could see three little boats anchored by a boat house at the end of another pier. My eyes were adjusting to the dark. I could even make out each mast. My mind took me back to a scorching day during my twelfth summer, which I spent sailing with Lydia's son and his wife. He took us out on Biscayne Bay, where the water was a crisp turquoise and the gulls screeched above our red and yellow sails and my heart was happy and free. The broiling sun had darkened Rafaelito's arms up to the generous armholes of his sleeveless undershirt to a deep *criollo* tan, leaving a permanent etching of the garment on his chest and shoulders. Seeing my amusement at his two-toned body, he had splashed a pail of refreshing salt water over me.

"Do they teach sailing here?"

"Yeah!" Justin glanced over his shoulder briefly. "It's considered P. E."

"I'd trade a classroom for this place in a minute."

I could make out the strands of his hair fluttering in the breeze and the corner of his mouth as it angled up in a smile.

"It's okay to tell me," I ventured to say. "There's no shame in it. My mom's been through it twice. First when she had to leave everything in Cuba and start from scratch, and a second time when my dad died."

"What are you talking about?"

"I suppose your parents fell into hard times and they couldn't afford this school anymore. Right?"

His eyes opened in surprise. "Nothing like that." He shook his head. "I'm sorry about your dad. Are you doing okay now?"

"I was only three when he died, so I wasn't aware of much. It was hard on my mom, I'm sure." He had raised my curiosity. Why would anyone leave such a great school? "You didn't cut it with your grades?"

Justin leaned back and laughed. "You're set on getting to the bottom of things. Well, I don't feel like talking about it. In fact I don't feel like talking at all."

I was keenly aware of his movements, as he drew one leg onto the dock and turned to face me. A shiver of apprehension rippled down my spine. I feared treading in the direction he was heading. I'd warned Susie that I wanted to avoid this type of awkward moment and she'd promised to stick by me. Now, I had no choice. Yet, when his hand brushed away a loose strand of hair from my temple, I didn't shy away.

His touch was light as a swallowtail's wing. "If we're really quiet, we'll hear it."

"We'll hear what?" A thread of wariness made my voice quiver.

"The music," he whispered, looking into my eyes. A pleasant warmth tickled my ear, as he brushed it with his fingertips.

"No way!" My words tumbled out through nervous giggles. "Bayside is miles away! There's no way you'd hear the band from here."

His lips curved in a soft smile, his eyes purposeful, unwavering. "The music of the breeze, of the waves . . ."

There was a kind of magic in what he said. I nodded, suddenly taken by the peace of the place.

His eyes caught and held mine. They probed into me. To my surprise, a wave of excitement broke my brief serenity. I challenged his gaze, then feared leading him to think there was much interest on my part. I knew I'd sent him a dangerous signal by hugging him during the game. Now, it was payback time, and I couldn't blame Susie for my dumb move. I dropped my lids to discourage him.

But the next thing I felt was the warmth of Justin's hand circling the back of my neck. He laced his fingers through my hair and drew me to him. A tingling warmth traveled over my skin. His lips touched mine gently, tentatively. He drew a soft breath. Then, as if energized by it, he pressed his lips lightly on my mouth again, molding to its contours and sending a surge of warmth through me.

Strangely, the thought crept into my mind that I had never been kissed by a boy wearing an earring. I couldn't help the smile that broke over my lips.

"What is it?" he whispered, his lips flicking mine with every word.

"Oh, nothing," I said, chuckling with embarrassment.

"I'm happy too." I felt his chest expand with a deep intake of air.

Though he worked hard to disguise it, I could tell from the trembling of his hands that the moment was awkward for him also. My mouth was no longer taut with a smile. I could taste the mint in his breath, as he touched his lips to mine, and was grateful he'd been so thoughtful.

"Maggie! Where are you?" Susie called from a distance.

"Justin! Maggie! Where did you go?" Carlos yelled.

Justin pulled away from me. "Damn!"

I laughed. "Should I answer them?"

"It would serve them right if we didn't. Their timing stinks!"

"Maggie!" Susie shouted.

"We're over here!" I yelled back to shore. "At the end of the dock!"

"How did you get there?"

I could see two dark shadows where the gentle waves broke on the other side of the fence.

"What the heck!" Two vertical lines of annoyance appeared between Justin's eyebrows. He got up and offering his hand, helped me to my feet. "Let's get back."

"We're coming!" I called back to Susie, as we collected our shoes and flashlight and started back. "Wait for us!"

"Don't worry. They're not going anywhere," Justin assured me. "I've got the keys. I'll bet they locked themselves out of the car"

I laughed. "Well, then, that's your revenge."

My laughter stopped abruptly when my toes plunged into the cold water. The thought of wading through the rocky darkness again sent a chill up my spine. This time, I had two more witnesses to my clumsy display. To add to my troubles, I was too proud to let my dread of the dark waters show.

Again, Justin took my hand and reassured me. "Take it easy. There's no rush."

"You have to wade around the fence in this darkness?" Fear clung to Susie's words. "Aren't you scared some creature will jump up and bite you?"

My heart lurched. A wave of panic froze me in place. I swayed precariously on one foot. Justin squeezed my hand tightly to steady me. *I really needed to hear that, Susie!* I wanted to yell, but I kept my sarcasm to myself.

"Thanks a lot!" he shouted over his shoulder. Then, softly he said to me, "Nothing's gonna hurt you. We're almost to the end of the fence."

I tried to force my legs to move again, but the fear of leaving the tested ground under each foot and exposing them again to another unexplored rock petrified me. Justin nudged me wrapping his other arm around me.

"It's okay," he whispered close to my ear. Then he turned to Carlos and yelled, "I'm throwing our shoes over the fence. Catch!"

He swung his moccasins one at a time and they landed safely on dry ground. He lobbed my sandals next, then slipped the flashlight into his pocket.

"Here, I'll carry you piggy-back."

I chuckled in embarrassment. "No way!"

Without discussion, he turned his back to me, bent forward slightly and commanded, "Climb on!"

He took long tentative strides with the extra burden. The water sloshed around his legs with every step. I worried that his feet would get cut on the jagged rocks and in pain, he'd send us both tumbling into the chilly waters. But he didn't seem affected by the rough terrain. In a few moments he had me back on safe ground and I slid off his back.

Susie ran up to me with my sandals. Holding on to her shoulder for balance, I brushed tiny rocks off my feet so I could get my shoes back on. When Justin gathered up his moccasins and stepped aside with Carlos, Susie and I had a moment alone.

"Wow!" Susie whispered excitedly. "I was afraid things were gonna get out of hand. I told Carlos we had to slow down."

My eyes widened. "I shouldn't have left you alone!"

She threw her hands up. "Nothing happened, I promise!" Then, she confided quietly, "But I sure like him, Maggie."

"You had me fooled." I slipped one shoe on, leaning against Susie's side. I took advantage of the few minutes the boys had given us. "Didn't he do well tonight?"

"He's been great! I think he really likes you."

"I hope you're right," I said dreamily. "I tried to wave, but I couldn't tell if he saw me."

"Nah, it's too dark. I think they have their backs to us."

I planted both feet on the ground and perched my hands on my hips. "Who are you talking about, Susie?" I asked her as loud as I dared. "You're mixing up Justin with Zach! It seems lately you have no clue what's going on!"

"How would I guess you're talking about Zach?" Susie snapped. "You've been with Justin all evening, *chica*. Talk about being clueless!"

"What are you getting at?"

"Justin's crazy about you!"

I glanced in the boys' direction for fear they'd heard us. Justin was coming our way. "He agreed to take me out on account of Carlos. That's all," I warned her confidentially. "Just like I gave in to help you out!"

"We gotta go!" There was a shade of urgency in Justin's voice. He grabbed my arm and started back.

Carlos rushed along too, pulling Susie behind him.

"What's going on?" I asked.

"I bet it's that pickup truck that showed up when we came looking for you," Susie said.

"It's just some kids from Masterson's. I hope they're not messing with my car."

I could see the boys in the shadows, four or five of them surrounding the Honda. I didn't like the looks of it.

"Get your hands off my car!" Justin fired off as we approached.

"Nobody's touching it," one sneered.

"This is private property, buddy!" another one yelled. The tense muscles of his arms and his balled fists threatened. "Unless you belong at Masterson's, you'd better get your butts out of here!"

"We're taking off!" Though I was certain he meant to appease them, there was a note of challenge to Carlos' voice.

The boys stood between us and the car, their legs spread apart, hands at the ready. My heart raced. I could tell from his straight shoulders and the set of his jaw, that Justin anticipated trouble. His hand tightened on my arm. I didn't complain, though it pinched painfully. He drew his car keys from his pocket and led me to the passenger door. As we walked past one of the boys, the chill of fear enveloped me.

"It's Bentley!" the boy on my right shouted. "He's back for more trouble!"

"You don't get it, do you?" A boy in a plaid shirt, who'd been checking out the back of the car, came around. "You're not welcome around here!"

Justin unlocked the door and shoved me into the front seat. I clicked the button for the back door and Susie slid in. Carlos stood guard by Susie's door. As Justin went to close my door, the boy in the plaid shirt kicked it shut. I was startled by the force of the blow.

"¡Ave María!" Susie prayed under her breath.

"Listen, Turner. I have no quarrel with you. Not anymore." Justin made a move to walk around the front of the car.

"Yeah, right!" the boy who kicked the door snarled. "You got the best of me because you played dirty! I won't let you get away with that again!"

Justin stopped for a moment. "I didn't play dirty! It was an accident and you know it."

"Maybe it's *your* turn to have an accident."

¡Dios mío! The skin on my neck prickled.

"Let the jerk have it! It's time you had a fair go at him!" one of the boy's friends shouted.

"We're right behind you, Turner," another one said, moving in closer.

Get in the car, Justin! Let's get out of here! a voice inside me kept screaming.

Justin didn't move a muscle. "You're real brave when you have a bunch of friends around. Aren't you, Turner?"

"I don't need their help to set you straight, buddy!"

"If I took you on this time, no way you'd mess with me again!"

I swung the door open. "Justin, no!"

Susie screamed, "Maggie, get back in!"

"Get back in the car, Maggie." Justin didn't take his eyes off Turner. "I'll handle this!"

"I don't know what's between you two," I spoke out, not allowing the hammering of my heart to make my voice quaver. "But I don't want to be caught in the middle of a fight."

Carlos cut in. "Let's get out of here, man. You don't need this crap."

I was glad to see Carlos take the sensible approach. When clearly outnumbered, there is only one face-saving way out: walk away.

Justin gave the one called Turner a daring stare. For a moment, my heart pounded for fear he'd made the wrong move. Finally, Justin turned his back to the waiting boys, rounded the front of the car and got in. I didn't release my breath until the engine started up and we backed onto the paved road.

Carlos slapped the back of Justin's head. "Geez, Man! Good way to end a date!"

Susie and I laughed nervously, but Justin only jerked his head to the side. The set of his jaw told me he was in no mood for jokes.

Chapter 6

Monday morning in German class, I eyed the empty desk to my right anxiously. The kids flowed into the room before the second bell, and I hoped Zach would show up before someone else took the seat. No way I'd admit I was saving it for him. Sometimes, to my complete dismay, Billy Jewell would plop down by me, leaving Zach no choice but to find whatever empty desk was left. When that happened, the hour of German class dragged on. Billy would mimic Mrs. Berger's instructions under his breath to get my attention. He'd make stupid faces like some middle-school clown. I fought to ignore Billy, aware that Zach had me in his range of vision as he sat a few rows behind.

Travel posters lined the walls above the blackboards with summer scenes of Germany and the Austrian Alps. A fine dust had settled over the tops where they buckled from humidity and age. But the centerpiece of the room, tacked on the front wall like a prize safari skin, was a pair of Lederhosen, the leather shorts with suspenders worn by Austrian boys. Rumor had it Mrs. Berger had worn the yellowed gray garment in her childhood.

Just as the second bell rang, Zach appeared at the door, spotted me and slid into the desk next to me.

My heart leaped, then raced. I gave him an easy smile.

"I made it," he whispered, a cocky glint in his eyes.

"She's gonna let you have it one day," I ventured, fearful of being heard by Mrs. Berger.

"Nah!" The toss of his chin accentuated his little dimple. "What page are we on?"

I put my finger by the page number and tipped my textbook in his direction.

Mrs. Berger read a few phrases and called on students to substitute the nouns. I practiced the words silently in case she picked me.

Mrs. Berger's wardrobe consisted of steel gray skirts and long-sleeved blouses, rolled to the elbow, as if ready to take on any challenge in the messy process of teaching us. Her bifocals pinched the wide bridge of her pink nose so tightly that I was sure she suffered oxygen deprivation. When reading, her chin came up, affording us a view into her red nostrils up to the dark depths of the clamped bridge. If she wanted our attention, her forehead dropped forward. Her piercing eyes focused on a selected student through the upper part of the lenses, which magnified and rounded her cobalt irises to extraterrestrial dimensions. The student was trapped in the unearthly gaze and prayed, wide-eyed, that his answer was correct.

After practicing the new vocabulary out loud, Mrs. Berger had us write out sentences in our notebooks using the new words. With a few minutes of class left, she granted us a treat. She had taught us a few German songs, and we got to sing them whenever she felt we'd accomplished what she planned for the hour. We welcomed the break from book work. Our renditions, though barely recognizable to a native German speaker and often off key, were belted out with gusto.

"Let's pair up so we can share the music books," Mrs. Berger announced.

Zach raised his eyebrows at me. "You wanna share?"

Yes, yes, yes! my heart said. I gave him a quick shrug. "If you want . . ."

He shoved his desk against mine and we held up the music book between us. I was dizzy with joy.

"Sorry about the game Friday," I said.

He pressed his lips together. "Yeah, that was pretty bad."

"I hated to see that foul called against you."

He eyed me with surprise. "You were there?"

He hadn't seen me. I'd made a fool of myself hugging Justin, and Zach hadn't even spotted me. I decided to give him something to think about. "A guy took me to the game."

He nodded. I searched his eyes for some hint of curiosity, but they revealed nothing.

"Open your books to page twenty-three," I heard Mrs. Berger say. "We'll sing *Die Lorelei*."

Zach rolled his eyes. I gave him a commiserating look, though I really did like the song.

Ich weiss nicht, was soll es bedeuten . . .

The key was too high for most boys. Their flat notes caused me to chuckle.

"I don't dare sing this one," Zach whispered to the tune.

"Hey, this is authentic stuff," I teased. If we timed it right, we appeared to be mouthing the German lyrics as we carried on a conversation.

Ein Märchen aus uralten Zeiten . . .

"I'm sure glad you work for Grams," Zach said.

I took a dry swallow. I didn't expect a disclosure of his feelings in the middle of class.

. . . das kommt mir nicht aus dem Sinn.

He cocked his head and glanced at me. "Now I know where to find myself a tutor for German."

"Sure," I whispered, the back of my neck tingly and warm.

"I'll stop by Gram's if we have something going in class. You know, a test or something."

Die Luft ist kühl, und es dunkelt . . .

"Anytime." My heart quickened. Zach was going to stop by Mrs. Maxwell's to spend time with me.

"If my grades drop below a C, I'll be kicked off the team."

I promised myself not to let that happen, at least not in German class. "I took her some Thanksgiving leftovers, Cuban-style, that is."

"You're kidding! Grams ate that stuff?"

Der Gipfel des Berges funkelt, im Abend sonnenschein.

I didn't like his tone. "Of course she did. She liked every-thing."

"She was being polite," he flashed me a teasing smile. My heart melted.

Die schönste Jungfrau sitzet . . .

"I bet you've never tried any Cuban food. Next time I take her something, I'll save you a bite."

Ihr gold'nes Geschmeide blitzet . . .

"I'll be out of town."

I no longer felt comfortable talking about Cuban food. "She showed me your baby pictures."

I thought I noticed a pink flush crawl across his freckled cheeks. "I hope she put away the bare-butt pictures."

I smiled wickedly and shook my head.

"She loves to embarrass me."

. . . sie kämmt ihr goldenes Haar.

"You had no hair until you were two?"

The grin pasted on his face didn't disguise the defensive note in his voice. "I had some."

It felt good to see I'd gotten to him. "Someone should've slapped some clothes on you and covered your head with a bon-net! Those pictures were *nasty!*"

"Thanks."

He reached under his seat for his chemistry book and spread it open on the desk. Then, he propped up the music book on the edge of the desk, hiding the chemistry text from Mrs. Berger's view.

"What are you doing?" I feared I'd blown it.

"I've got a quiz in my next class. Hold up the music book for me, will you?"

Ich glaube, die Wellen verschlingen
am Ende noch Schiffer und Kahn . . .

I joined the class in song for the last stanza, while balancing the music book upright and watching him uneasily from the corner of my eye. We had been getting along so well. Why did I go and tease him?

"Do we have time for another song?" A girl asked.

"Let's sing *Wenn die Soldaten*," a few of the boys shouted.

Mrs. Berger scanned the room. "You'll get me in trouble stomping your feet on the floor like you always do."

"It's a marching song, Mrs. Berger," Billy Jewell shouted. "We like to act it out."

Mrs. Berger set her eyes, extraordinarily magnified by the lenses, on Zach. "*Herr* Sherwood!"

Zach looked up from his reading. "*Bitte?*"

Her red nostrils flared. "*Was ist das auf ihrem Schreibtisch?*"

He looked lost. His face turned a fiery red.

"What've you got on your desk?" I whispered, my lips stiff and wooden.

"*Das ist mein* . . . chemistry book," he stammered.

I could hear a few muffled chuckles.

"In German class you study German, *Herr* Sherwood." She shoved up a sleeve. "Put that book away."

He slammed the book shut, disgust oozing from his eyes.

I joined the class for our last song, mercifully interrupted by the bell. We gathered our packs and filed out of the room.

"Thanks for getting me out of that one," Zach said behind me.

"Sure, anytime."

As I merged into the flow of kids streaming down the hall I saw Kelly Rogers working her way in the opposite direction. She wore a blue top that clung to her like an outer skin. Her eyes searched the crowd.

I took a few more steps and stole a look behind me. Kelly had her hand on Zach's arm, and her eyelashes fluttered like spastic moths. The knot that formed in my stomach was hardly from hunger pangs.

Zach had teased me heartlessly and now he wasn't fighting off the girl's nervy advances. I began to wonder about the jasmine's happy prediction this morning.

Disgusted, I turned around to continue down the hall, but I found my path blocked by Justin, who had appeared at my side from among the throng of kids.

"Heading over to Geometry?" he asked.

I was surprised he could keep track of my schedule. "Yep," I said, rearranging the shoulder strap of my backpack. "To see Mr. Skinny Tie, who hasn't learned that the hypotenuse of his tie is too narrow."

Justin's teeth sparkled when he laughed. "Poor Mr. Sutter. Someone's got to bring him up to date." He started to break through the mob of students. "I'll walk you there."

"I don't want to make you late to your next class." I tried to set aside my anger over Kelly.

"It's on my way. I won't be late." He shrugged. Despite his assurance, he appeared nervous and hesitant. "Look, I wanted to let you know I had a good time Friday."

"I did too," I answered almost too quickly.

His lips broke into a wide smile. "Hey, do you want to get some lunch together at break?"

I panicked to think I might run into Zach when I was with another boy. "No. I can't." My thoughts were racing to come up with a plausible excuse. I didn't want to hurt Justin's feelings. "I brought my lunch today."

"So? Can it! It's my treat."

I shook my head. "I'm planning to study for a quiz during lunch." I grabbed the door knob to my classroom. "Thanks anyway."

"Whatever," I heard him mutter under his breath.

Though I was annoyed that Kelly Rogers stuck to Zach like guava jelly, I knew I didn't have much of a claim on him. At least not yet. I rehearsed different ways of setting her straight, to be prepared for when the time was right. But by the end of the day, she was no longer taking up my personal time. My heart fluttered with anticipation on my way to Mrs. Maxwell's home that afternoon. I wondered when Zach would take me up on my offer to help him. We'd had no German homework for the day, yet irrationally, I had expected his Bronco would be parked in front of her house. When I rounded the corner, I confirmed it wasn't. Still, I fanned a flicker of hope that he'd stop by later.

"I could set my watch by your visits, Maggie. Always prompt." Mrs. Maxwell closed the door behind me. "Did you have a good day at school?"

"Pretty good." I dropped my purse on the couch and followed her into the kitchen. "Zach wants me to help him with German. He says he'll drop by your house whenever we have a test or something."

"That figures!" Mrs. Maxwell said. "I hardly see hair or hide of that boy. But once he finds out there's a pretty girl coming to my house everyday, he wants to visit."

I felt the color rush to my face. I was glad the timing bell for the dryer went off and she got busy with the laundry.

"Oh, no, Mrs. Maxwell," I said when she started piling the dry clothes into a basket. "You shouldn't bend down like that. I'll take those out for you."

"I do this kind of work all the time, sweetie," she assured me, holding on to the side of the appliance with one hand and reaching into the hot opening with the other. "It's no big deal."

I worked my way between the dryer and the basket. "That's what you hired me for. Remember?"

"I didn't hire you to do the laundry, Maggie," she said, though she gave me room to work. "I hired you to keep me company."

"And to help you," I insisted.

"To keep an eye on me is closer to the truth, if you ask my daughter and Dr. Stevens." I couldn't help smiling when she laughed. She propped her cane against the wall and sat at the kitchen table. "Hand me some of the clothes and I'll start folding them."

I gathered a few things for her, then emptied the dryer and joined her at the table to fold.

"What I want is for you to run over to the grocery store. I put together a list of things I need."

Normally, that was an errand I loved. Susie and I chatted while she bagged groceries. But today, I was afraid Zach would show up at the house and I'd miss him. More likely, he'd walk in while I was smoothing out one of his grandmother's lace bras. If that happened, I'd bolt out the door and move to China. "I'll help you finish this load of laundry, then I'll go," I said.

"Do you suppose they'd sell any Cuban dishes at the store?"

"Ready made?" I glanced up from the satiny slip I was folding. "I don't think so."

"I made two meals out of those goodies you brought me." Mrs. Maxwell turned a pair of nylon panties right side out. "It was so nice of you to think of me. Everything was delicious. Give your mom my compliments."

"I will," I said, unable to look her in the eye. I remembered Zach had doubted she'd like the food and I feared she was only being kind.

"I enjoyed the turkey. It had the most exotic flavor."

"I warned you about Cuban food," I apologized. "We use a lot of herbs and stuff."

"And that thing like a potato . . ."

"The *yuca?*"

"Goodness! That was tangy."

"It's the *mojo*, the spicy sauce we put on it, that gives it flavor, or else the *yuca* would be very bland. It's made with olive oil, garlic, onions and sour orange."

"Do you know how to make it? Maybe you can buy the ingredients for me."

"I help my mom, but I don't really know the amounts and the timing and all."

"Well then, you're going to have to ask your mom to send me some leftovers at Christmas. I'd really love to have that *yooc-ah* again."

"You really liked it?" I looked into her serene blue eyes this time.

"Would I ask you to bring me something I wouldn't eat?"

I chuckled. "I'll tell her. But she won't be able to cook this Christmas. She's got to work on Christmas day."

"Oh, my! And you're going to be all alone?" Mrs. Maxwell didn't give me time to answer. "We won't have that. You're spending Christmas with us at my daughter's house."

I couldn't hold back a gasp. Zach and I together on Christmas day! My head was a whirlwind of thoughts. I wished I hadn't rushed to ask Susie to have me over. How could I turn Susie down now? "Well, I . . ."

"Oh, I didn't think. Maybe you've made other plans?"

My heart raced. "No. Not really."

"Then, it's settled. I'll let my daughter know you're joining us."

Susie was busy bagging a load of groceries when I walked into Publix. She had her back to the door. I made a mental note to avoid mentioning Christmas. It would be a delicate matter to tell Susie about the change in plans. Breaking plans with your best friend required timing and finesse to keep from crushing her ego like an eggshell. I came up behind her and poked her side.

She squirmed and laughed. "Hey, I'm glad to see you! Are you shopping for Mrs. Maxwell or for home?"

"Mrs. Maxwell sent me. You look cute in your orange Publix golf shirt."

"Excuse me!" Susie plucked at the store name embroidered on the shirt. "The shirt's peach, the logo teal. It must be nice to be hiking around town and getting paid for it."

"Hey!" I shrugged, looking around for a grocery wagon. "This is part of my job."

"Some kinda nursing! If you hear of any other recuperating patient, I'll take the job."

"I promise the next one's yours." I rolled an empty wagon back by her side. "I'll look for you when I come back to the register."

"Great! I'll bag your things and we'll talk. Is there a lot on your list?"

"Just as much as I can carry."

She gave me a sassy wink. "Mrs. Maxwell should've called her grandson to take you shopping."

I laughed. "Right."

I swept through the entire store, rounding some of the stands and displays more than once, to find all the items on the list. This was one of those times I wished I possessed Mami's mental map of every aisle and its grocery residents. Mami said she'd gained the knowledge from years of practice. She shopped at least twice a week. On Mondays, she ran by El Gallo for their freshly delivered Caribbean produce to make sure she'd get the ripest plantains and plumpest *boniatos,* and for all the other

Cuban specialties that Publix didn't carry. On Thursdays, she'd take advantage of sale prices at Publix and buy canned goods, pasta and American goodies, like chips and dip, which El Gallo didn't bother to stock. If I mentioned to her the trouble I had finding my way around, she'd assign me that shopping as another one of my chores.

My first stop was the cosmetic aisle, where I got clear nail-polish for Mrs. Maxwell and picked out Mystic Mauve for myself. I had little trouble finding the whole-wheat bread, green and red peppers, garlic, and lettuce. Those were easy to spot. But finding coffee filters, teabags, celery seed and a bay-scented candle sent me on a twenty-minute trek through the maze of displays. These items were hardly ever found in a Cuban home. What did she want with a bay-scented candle, anyway? In the paper aisle, I glanced around discretely to make sure no one saw me picking out aqua toilet paper. I prayed I'd beat Zach to Mrs. Maxwell's, so he wouldn't catch me putting it away. I grabbed the December issue of *Southern Living* and headed for the dairy section. Only one item on the list was heavy, the skim milk, and mercifully Mrs. Maxwell had requested only a half-gallon.

The cashier I selected was a middle-aged woman with hollow cheeks and swift fingers. She wore an award pin on her teal vest that read: *Serving you is my pleasure.* As I unloaded the groceries onto the turntable at the register Susie called to me.

"Would you like paper or plastic, Miss?" She held up two bags.

"Plastic, please," I answered in a most refined manner and tilted my nose in the air. "And, make sure you don't crush the bread, bruise the lettuce or spill the polish. Don't put the milk in with the magazine. It will sweat. And don't bag the candle with the coffee filters. It will stink them up."

The cashier gave me a suspicious glance.

"Anything else, Miss?" Susie asked, unable to control a burst of giggles.

"Yes, would you please get me a six pack of beer?"

"You don't look twenty-one to me, young lady." The cashier's eyes pierced mine. "I can't sell beer to a minor."

"She's just goofing off, Louise. This is my best friend, Maggie."

"Hello!" I smiled, but Louise seemed to have locked up her sense of humor in the store safe.

"I figured something was up," Louise said.

"Would you ring up this nail polish separately?" I held up the small bottle.

Her mouth shriveled like a raisin, but she ran it through the scanner. I raised my brow at Susie. Susie pressed her lips and shrugged.

"That'll be two sixty-eight," the woman told me.

I handed her the exact amount for my purchase.

"Maggie's celebrating Christmas at my house," Susie told the woman, then looked in my direction. "Mamá loved the idea."

My throat tightened. "Oh, you didn't. You asked your mom already?"

"Of course! Were you planning to show up her Christmas Eve with your pillow under your arm and watch her jaw drop like an overheated iguana's?"

The scanner beeped as the cashier rang up Mrs. Maxwell's groceries.

"No, of course," I said, buying time to think. "But Susie, you didn't give me much time to clear it up with Mami's friends. You know . . . What if they insist?"

"Phew!" Susie dismissed the whole thing with a wave of her hand. "When has that ever stopped you, Maggie Castillo?"

I must have had a look of despair in my eyes, because Susie frowned. "Is there something you're not telling me? You don't want to spend Christmas with me? It was your idea, Maggie."

"Yes, I know."

Susie had stopped bagging. Her hands went to her hips. "What's going on, *chica?*"

"*I* don't know what's going on," the cashier interrupted. "But *you* owe me twenty-five thirty-nine." Then, she pointed a finger at Susie. "And *you* had better start packing up her things."

I paid with Mrs. Maxwell's folded bills. I kept my eyes down and was sure the cashier thought I was being meek on her account, because she thanked me nicely after counting out the change. But it was Susie whose eyes I feared meeting.

"Come on. I'll walk you out to your car," Susie said, her hands on the wagon handle.

"You'll walk me to my—?" It took me a moment to understand what she meant. "Oh, sure. Help me put the bags in the trunk."

Heading out of the store, I lagged a few steps behind Susie and made a big deal of wrestling with the zipper of my purse while I put the change back. I had to figure how to explain things to Susie. "Five more minutes with that woman and I would've ripped the cashier's pin off her uniform. Did you see what it said?" I asked her.

The way she tossed her head warned me she wasn't interested. "Nah."

"It said she's happy to serve you, something like that. She's not happy today! What's with her?"

Susie slowed down, forcing me to walk by her side. "Who cares?"

"She probably doesn't get enough to eat!" I laughed. I could see Susie's light mood was gone. The corner of her lip went up in a sneer. "I feel for you, having to work with her all day."

"I can put up with it for a few hours. What I can't stand is when you keep stuff from me." Susie's dark eyes dug into mine. "Let's get back to Christmas. What's going on?"

All my efforts at finesse had to be scrapped. "Mrs. Maxwell invited me to her daughter's on Christmas day."

"And you told her you had other plans. Right?"

"She didn't give me a chance," I rattled off loudly in self-defense. "It was all so sudden. With Mami working and no family in Miami, I guess she figured I had no place to go. She's so sweet, I couldn't find the words to say no."

We had rounded the side of the building, where Susie could no longer be seen from inside the store and she could spare a few minutes to talk. She pushed the wagon aside and perched her hands on her hips. "You found them for me."

"You're my best friend, Susie. I'm supposed to be able to tell you anything."

"Then be honest with me, *chica*. You're breaking our plans because you'd rather be with Zach."

I bit back a smile. "Wouldn't you?"

"Not after what Carlos said about him. If the guy doesn't like Cubans, that's the last place I'd spend Christmas."

And unspoken agreement between best friends gave us permission to be ruthlessly blunt with each other. But that didn't prevent me from feeling a prick of annoyance. "Zach's grandmother likes me, and she said I'd be welcome. Besides, who cares what Carlos thinks?"

Susie's brow furrowed with anger. "*I* care!"

"If it were you, you'd break our plans and spend Christmas with him."

"Not for Zach." She looked away, her lips tightly drawn her brow wrinkled into a frown. Then, an impish smile broke through. "I would for Carlos."

I hugged her, laughing with relief. "I knew you'd understand."

"I suppose . . ." We stepped aside for a car that was driving through the parking lot. Then, with studied indifference, she said, "*Oye,* the guys want to take us out again."

"Justin and Carlos?" No wonder she'd been understanding about Christmas. "Not again!"

"Why not?" Susie grabbed my arm and made me face her, quizzing me with an intense look. "You had a good time Friday. Didn't you?"

A little wave of excitement traveled up my spine, when I remembered the warmth of Justin's kiss. "It was okay," I answered softly. "But I sure didn't have a good feeling when those boys showed up. Seems to me, Justin's got a fondness for fights."

"If that was the case, Maggie, he'd have thrown the first punch. I think he was pretty much in control."

"That's because he's no fool. He was outnumbered." I shook my head. "They kept bringing up some other fight they'd had. I don't like to get involved in that sort of thing. Who knows what he's been up to? Maybe it's gang revenge or some other mess. We hardly know the guy."

"Gangs at Masterson's? Give me a break, Maggie."

"I bet that's why he was kicked out of Masterson's. He probably beat up someone."

Susie shrugged. "I don't know what happened." Then, her eyes twinkled in challenge. "If you feel you hardly know Justin, give him another chance. Let's go out with the guys again!"

"That's not going to happen, Susie." I looked squarely at her and ventured into dangerous territory. "Aren't you moving a little too fast with this guy?"

"What? A second date is fast?"

"How well do you know Carlos?"

Susie eyed me with suspicion. "I suppose you're mad at Carlos for telling you what he thinks?"

"No matter what I say about Carlos, you're gonna take it the wrong way."

Her chin rose and her eyes took on a cocky squint. "I can take it, whatever it is."

Her assurance didn't satisfy me, I figured I'd end up hurting her feelings. But we'd boarded a runaway train of brutal honesty and our friendship dangled from its caboose. Was it loyalty or retaliation that was powering its engine? I didn't take the time to figure it out.

I'd had an unsettling feeling about whatever it was Carlos wanted from Susie. He'd been moving too fast. I didn't see him taking time learn what was important to Susie, or practicing the delicate task of pleasing the person you care about. I'd never shared my misgivings for fear she'd think I was jealous of his time with her. Now, as she shoved Justin into my life, she triggered the Cuban brashness in me. "What does he want from you? Have you had a long talk?"

"We've talked." She shrugged defensively. "He likes me. A lot. He wants me to go out with him only."

"And, do you think he respects you?"

"You sound like my mother."

"Be on your toes, okay?"

"I can take care of myself." Her dark eyes burned into mine. "You're green with envy. You wish this was the way things were rolling for you and Zach!"

"Oh, Susie. Your cables are crossed. You're so swept away by this guy, you can't even take advice from a friend."

"Thanks!" Her eyes burned with sarcasm. "There! I accept your advice."

"I'm just worried for you."

"I can take care of myself." She tossed her hair back in a gesture of defiance, then went back to her prime goal. "So, will you give Justin another chance?"

"My heart's not in it, really. I don't want to ruin things with Zach."

"Give it a rest, Maggie!"

From her tone, I gathered she didn't give much credibility to my chances with Zach. I was hurt. "Okay. Who's not being honest now? You don't care how I feel about Zach or Justin. All you care about is seeing Carlos."

"Maybe so. But at least he's been asking me out."

"And what is that supposed to mean?"

"Look, I don't want to hurt you. Maybe Zach does like you. But you're lapping up every crumb he throws your way like a homeless puppy."

Though at first I felt Susie was paying me back for sharing my doubts about Carlos' intentions, pinholes of doubt began to appear in my confidence. Zach *had* been playing it cool. I thought I had read his signals correctly, but lately, Kelly Rogers' presence had raised a warning flag. I hoped that Christmas at Zach's would put a new spin on things. Maybe he was waiting for a moment alone at his place to ask me out. Susie's tactless honesty raised the stubborn streak in me. I wouldn't let on that she'd given me reason to worry. "I'll be a puppy wagging my tail along Zach's trail as long as I choose. It's my life!"

"You're blind."

A rift was splitting our friendship. It saddened me. I couldn't allow us to be angry over boys. It was too silly. The moment had arrived to set my pride aside. "How long have we been friends?"

"Before we could even speak English. Dumb question!"

"So, we're gonna sweep our friendship out over some stupid boys?"

I waited for her answer half in anger, half in dread. Susie's breath, coming in short grunts of annoyance, didn't mask the debate that I was sure raged in her head as it did in mine.

Susie nodded. "You're right." She gave me a slow smile. "Except for the *stupid* stuff. Carlos is not stupid."

I chuckled. "All boys are!"

Chapter 7

Susie's mom dropped us off at the mall the Saturday before Christmas. We bought presents for our families and split up for a few minutes to buy something for each other. This year, I had added Mrs. Maxwell to my shopping list. We browsed through the garden departments looking for a special terra-cotta planter or a hand-painted watering can. But when I saw a fringed cotton throw blanket woven with potted flower designs, I knew it was just the right gift for her.

When we finished at the mall, Mami picked us up and took us to my house. Susie and I were wrapping gifts in my bedroom when Mami tapped on the door. "There's two boys at the front door asking for you."

"What boys?" Boys at my front door were as rare as mangoes at Christmas.

Mami raised her eyebrows and shrugged.

"It's Carlos and Justin." Susie jumped up from the floor and headed out of the bedroom.

I grabbed her arm. "How do you know who it is? Did you ask them to stop by?"

Susie wriggled her arm free. "I'm just guessing, Maggie."

She wouldn't look me in the eye. "How do they know we're here?"

"Come on, *chica*. They know where you live," she whispered. "I guess they showed up."

"Hi Mag, Suze!" Carlos waved a hand in greeting.

Justin, who stood behind him on the porch, glanced at me, gave me a little nod and immediately began to study the blossoms on the jasmine vine. There was a raw bulge over his left eye and I thought I could detect a bluish tint around it. I figured he'd been in a fight and found myself pursing my lips in disapproval.

"Did you get your shopping done?" Carlos asked.

I stared hard at Susie, but her eyes were locked on Carlos. "We just got back from the mall."

"What are you up to?" he asked.

"We were wrapping presents in Maggie's room." Her voice rose with a little girl's sweetness when she talked to Carlos.

"We're going back to Just's to shoot pool." Carlos coiled a strand of Susie's hair around his finger. "Wanna hang around?"

"Sure!"

I hated when she answered for the both of us without consulting me. I gave her a smoldering look. "What about the gift wrapping?"

Carlos swatted his hand in the air, giving little importance to my concerns. "It's Saturday night, Mag. You can do that some other time."

Mami came to the door. "What's happening?"

"The boys want us to go over to Justin's." Susie sported a radiant smile. "Have you met Carlos and Justin, Mrs. Castillo?"

"I remember you went out together the other night," Mami said. "Hello boys." Carlos and Justin took turns shaking hands with Mami. I was glad she didn't mention the bruise around Justin's eye. I'd be embarrassed if she probed and gave him nursing advice. Instead, she put her arm around my shoulder. "I think that's a great idea. You're out of school for Christmas break. Go out and have fun."

I gave her a sickly smile, grabbed Susie's purse and mine and left with them.

I didn't dare look at the backseat as Justin drove to his house. As soon as we got into the car, Susie and Carlos were murmuring sweet things to each other. It made the skin of my neck crawl.

Justin's house had a high-columned entrance and semicircular glass panels above the windows, which reminded me of sliced oranges. It was designed in the modern Florida style popular in the western end of town: tall on ceilings and short on backyards. I'd said my good-byes to many Cuban friends, whose families had left our older neighborhood for new homes. The houses were so tightly fitted in the lots that, when the neighbors sneezed, the kids caught the germs. I preferred the aromas of family memories recorded in an older home, the sweet scent of scarred oak floors, the balmy essence of years of home cooked-meals, the mingled fragrances of baby powder and after-shave. And I wouldn't give up my big back yard, where we'd planted tropical fruits and fragrant shrubs. But Justin's lot wasn't skimpy and I was pleased to see that someone in his family also had a good hand with plants. Tall skinny palms flanked each side of the door. Clumps of liriope, pink begonias and elephant ears were tucked in little islands under the taller landscaping.

Justin led us through the white-tiled living area, our footsteps echoing through the sparsely furnished rooms. He switched on lights as we entered each room.

"Where's your mom and dad?" I asked warily.

"They went out." Justin opened the blinds which covered the windows of the family room. The aquamarine water of the swimming pool beyond shimmered like a jewel when the underwater lights came on.

"We have the house to ourselves, girls!" Carlos rubbed his hands together, sending a cold prickle down my spine.

Susie was examining a stand of cue sticks on the wall. She held a stick and gauged it for balance.

"Have you ever shot pool, Suze?"

"My uncle has a pool table." Susie's eyes took on the captivated look of a newborn fawn. "I've tried it a few times."

"Have you?" Justin asked me softly.

"Nope."

"Great!" Carlos rubbed chalk on the end of the cue stick he'd picked. "Let's play a round. Me and Suze against you and Mag. I'm gonna kick your butts!"

"Don't be so sure, bud." Justin turned his Dolphins cap around, so that the bill covered the back of his neck.

"With my skill, and knowing that Mag has never held a stick in her hand, it'll be a breeze." Carlos' smile had a cocky cant to it.

I stood by the green felt-lined table, with my arms crossed over my chest. No one had asked my opinion.

Justin gave him a self-assured laugh. "Tell you what." He handed me a stick. I didn't want Carlos to notice I didn't know how to hold it in my hand. "I'll give Maggie directions and I'm so sure we'll win, that I'll bet you a pizza. Loser pays."

"You're on," said Carlos, as Justin set up the balls with the triangular rack. "I'll break."

Carlos hit the white ball hard and it smashed against the others, scattering them all over the table. One of the striped balls went down a pocket. He pumped his fist. "Yes!"

Then, he took aim at another. He leaned down, hit the white ball, which in turn tapped one of the striped ones. The ball rolled slowly and stopped short of the pocket.

"You go first, Maggie," Justin said. "Pick out a solid ball and send it into a pocket by smacking it with the cue ball."

"The what?" I could hear Carlos snickering behind me when I asked the question.

Justin smiled. "The cue ball is the white ball."

"Got ya."

I figured he wanted to give me a turn while there were so many options on the table. Still, I wasn't sure what to do.

"Start by aiming for that solid yellow ball. Put your left hand on the table, like this." His fingers made a little pedestal to rest the stick and I followed his directions. "Now, hook your index finger over the stick so it can slide through it."

Apparently, I was putting too much pressure on the hooked finger, because he placed his hand over mine. His warm touch sent goose pimples up my arm. "Hold it lightly," he said, his shoulder touching mine, his voice very close to my ear. "Now, I want you to remember what you learned in geometry."

I cast a puzzled look over my shoulder, and to my discon-cert, Justin's lips landed on my cheek. Making the most of the moment, he gave me a light peck. My heart pounded.

"Ooh!" Susie crooned. "I saw that!"

"Oh, stop it, Susie!" I didn't intend to respond so harshly, but it was hard to remain composed when a rush of confused emotions swirled inside me. I took a breath of relief when Justin continued giving me directions.

"Picture a line from the pocket you're aiming for to your solid ball. The cue ball should hit your solid ball where the imaginary line crosses it. So, if you want to go for the yellow ball, where do you want to hit it?"

"Right here," I said, pointing at a spot on the ball.

"Go for it," Justin said, stepping aside.

The cue ball bounced off the yellow ball and sent it into the nearest pocket.

"Wow!" said Susie.

"I'd go for this one now." Justin pointed to a red ball.

I sent the second ball into a pocket too.

From the corner of my eye, I could see Carlos shake his head. "Beginner's luck," he said.

"Great coaching," Justin corrected him. Justin pointed again. "This green one is your best bet now, Maggie."

I took aim, but my confidence must have been flying to the heavens. This time, the ball I intended to hit didn't make it into the pocket, but the cue ball did.

It was Susie's turn. She placed her hand on the table, but instead of looping her finger over the stick, she used her fingers as a living tripod.

"You won't have any control if you don't hook your finger over the stick," Carlos reproached her.

Susie batted her lashes at him. "This is how I learned to play."

"Well it's not the best way," Carlos insisted.

"Let her shoot her way," Justin piped in. "You're breaking your partner's concentration."

Carlos shook his head. When Susie's ball failed to roll into the pocket, he shut his eyes and shook it again.

Justin showed me what he intended to do every time before he took aim. He got two balls in before he lost his turn.

Carlos picked up his stick with a cocky smirk across his face. But when he sent one of his balls into the pocket and the cue ball followed, his lips had creased angrily.

We continued taking turns. I was enjoying the game much more than I'd expected, in part because Justin and I held a lead. But when my turn rolled around once more, I felt the pressure. Justin explained that I had one more solid ball to sink and after that one, I was to go for the black ball, the eight ball. If I got them into the pockets in that order without dropping the cue ball or one of our opponents' balls, we would win the game. The problem was that a striped ball blocked my path to the solid one. Susie listened attentively to Justin's directions, as Carlos paced at the other end of the table.

"Now, pretend I'm Mr. Skinny Tie going over angles in class."

I glanced up at Susie and we laughed. "You have a lot more hair on your head."

Justin patted the cap on his head. "Good thing." Then, he continued. "The cue ball will rebound off the side at the same angle as it hits it. So, determine where you want the ball to end up, and estimate the angle you want. That way you can avoid hitting their ball."

I studied the situation for a few moments. Then I laid the stick on the table. "I want it to go from here to here."

I looked up at Justin and he nodded. "So, where are you going to hit the solid ball?"

I scrunched my face. "On this spot?"

Justin smiled. "You got it."

I aimed and shot. The ball hit the side and bounced off in line with the solid ball, striking it and sending it in the pocket. I felt a glow of accomplishment rise to my face.

Justin slapped his thigh. "She's a natural!"

Carlos didn't say a word.

When the cue ball came to rest, my path to the eight ball was also blocked.

"Another shot like that, and we've got the game." Justin gave me a thumbs-up and laughed.

I traced the path I wanted, so that the cue ball would glance off the black ball and send it into a side pocket. Justin gave me a nod of approval and I prepared to shoot.

My mouth opened in amazement, as the balls responded to my shot just as I had intended. The thud of the eight ball dropping into the pocket was a bell of victory in my ear.

Justin put an arm around me and squeezed me. "You did it, partner!"

"Wow!" Susie said. "What other secrets are you keeping from me?"

I shrugged, though I couldn't help the contented smile on my face. "I've never played before."

"Pizza time!" Justin shouted.

Carlos grabbed the rack and began to gather the balls into it. "That was a practice game. Now, we'll go for the deciding round."

"No way!" Justin laughed, shoving the phone at Carlos. "Pepperoni, sweet peppers and mushrooms on a large pizza for me and Maggie. That's what you like, right, Maggie?"

I bit my lip to keep from cracking up with laughter, as my gaze darted to Carlos. "Perfect."

Carlos tried to act as though he wasn't bothered by the loss, but his expressive brows gave away his feelings. His irritation also came through as he ordered the pizza. "Pepperoni, sweet peppers and mushrooms," he growled through clenched teeth. "No, not *green* peppers! I said *sweet* peppers!"

Susie, Justin and I looked at each other and burst out laughing.

"Do you have any beer in the house?" Carlos asked Justin after hanging up.

I gave Susie a warning glance, and she pressed her lips innocently.

"No. There isn't any," Justin said, sticking his head in the refrigerator. "There's some Cokes and I found some chips."

"Let's take them to your room." Carlos grabbed two of the cold cans and, as though she was his possession, he wrapped an arm around Susie and led her. "We want to check out your home space."

I followed them down a dark hallway, turning and passing a few doors before we stopped. All the while I tried to rip open a bag of chips Justin had handed me. Carlos fumbled in the dark for the switch on a lamp. Instead of wallpaper, the far wall of Justin's room was covered in blue denim, as were the pillows on his full-size bed. I was surprised a blue and white comforter covered the bed without a wrinkle. I had always heard that boys didn't take the time to make their beds. Tabs from a sailcloth valance were looped around the handle of a wooden oar. And on one wall, among posters of his favorite bands, hung a six-string wood guitar.

Setting their soda cans on the windowsill, Carlos flopped down on the bed, made a mound of the pillows and lay back on them. Then he reached for Susie's hand and pulled her close, until she sat on the edge by his side.

I chose the chair by the desk, where I felt safe from any advances Justin might have in mind. After shutting the mess in his closet from view, he sat on a pile of schoolbooks stacked on the floor by the desk.

Seeing that I was still struggling with the bag of chips, Justin took it from me and snapped it open. "Now do you see how math can come in handy?"

"Sure," I said, grinning and reaching in the bag for a few chips. "It's real useful if you're majoring in billiards."

Justin smiled back. "So maybe you can't make a living out of shooting pool."

"You mean, like Carlos?" Susie teased.

Carlos gathered her hair in one hand and pulled her back.

"Ouch!" she cried.

"Yeah! I hope he's not planning to pay for the pizza with his winnings." Justin reached forward and slapped Carlos' leg. "Anyway, I think you'll enjoy geometry now that you found a use for it."

"Some of that was physics too, bud." The tone of Carlos' voice told me he was still sore.

"Can you play the guitar?" Susie attempted to get up to take a closer look, but Carlos pulled her down by the hair again. She swatted him. "Stop it!"

"Yeah. My cousin Randy taught me." Justin stuffed a handful of chips in his mouth and tiny crumbs stuck to his bottom lip. He cleaned them up with the tip of his tongue. "After a bunch of lessons, he said I played better than he did, so he gave it to me."

Susie reached for the bag of chips Justin was offering and cradled a few in her hand. "Will you play something for us?"

Carlos locked his arms around her from behind. "I don't think so. We've got other plans." He nibbled at Susie's ear, making her let out a cascade of giggles.

Trying to ignore their antics, I got busy inspecting the stuff on Justin's desk. My eyes were drawn to a dry brown blossom paperclipped to the lamp shade. I reached for it. "What's this?"

Justin's eyes opened wide. "It's nothing."

I had seen plenty of jasmine blossoms after they'd dried out and fallen to the ground. This was a jasmine from my vine. No question about it. I wondered how he'd gotten it, then remembered I'd left one in his car the night we went out. Next to the lamp, among a bunch of doodles on the denim wall, he'd jotted my phone number. Susie was right. Justin liked me. A curl of excitement made my heart race.

Carlos was kissing Susie. The potato chips had tumbled from her hand onto her lap and the plaid comforter. Justin and I sat, stiff as soldiers at attention forced to watch the intimate demonstration. We were too shy to talk to each other after my discovery of the jasmine; too embarrassed to sit and stare at the other two.

I exhaled a breath from deep inside. My discomfort must have been noticeable, because Susie took the time to ask me, "What's with you?"

Carlos grimaced before I could answer. "You know. She thinks Just is a hot-head and she doesn't like guys who fight."

Susie had told him what I'd shared with her. "Susie!"

"Well?" She seemed unconcerned at my discomfort. I couldn't understand how she could be a different person when she was around Carlos. "You might as well be honest, *chica*. Let the guy know how you feel."

Justin's hand went to the bump above his eye.

"I guess that's been bothering me," I said quietly, accepting that the word was out. "Those guys who came after you the other night and something they said about another fight you'd had . . . Now a black eye. I just don't know."

"I bet she thinks you were kicked out of Masterson's for fighting," Carlos said.

Justin rubbed the ball of his foot into the carpet.

"She's right, anyway." Carlos egged him on. "Why don't you let her know what happened?"

Justin grabbed my hand and stormed out of the room. "Come on."

We sat on a lounge chair by the pool. The air was fresh, dry and cool, as it was most winter nights in Miami. Though I didn't think it was right to leave Susie and Carlos alone in the bedroom, I was glad to be away from them, to breathe freely without them in my face. Susie had completely fallen for him. But Carlos didn't seem to treat her as though he really cared. At least, that was not the way I wanted a guy to treat me.

"Look, the truth is I got kicked out of Masterson's for fight-ing. I broke Turner's arm." Justin glanced at me for a reaction. He seemed to be testing me. I didn't know what to say.

"I thought you'd run out the door if I told you that." Justin chuckled. "There's more to the story."

"I figured there was."

"I'd been dating this girl named Tess. One day she ran across a set of the biology questions before a test. I didn't want any part of it. It's not that I'm so clean, but I didn't need help with the subject and I wasn't about to take a chance and be kicked out of school." He winced. "Look where it got me in the end."

I smiled and waited for him to continue.

"In spite of what I told her, I guess Tess wanted to get on my good side by helping me. When she finished with her cheat-sheet, she crumpled it up into a ball and lobbed it under her desk at my feet. For a moment, I froze. I was angry at her and scared to be caught with the hot sheet. So, when Mr. Nolan, our teacher, wasn't looking, I kicked it away from me. The wad of paper caught Mr. Nolan's eye as it landed by Turner's desk. Mr. Nolan picked it up, saw what it was and ripped up Turner's test."

"Didn't he deny knowing anything about it?"

"Of course. But he was so nasty about claiming his inno-cence that Mr. Nolan sent him to the dean."

"Did anyone tell on Tess?"

"No one else knew it was her cheat-sheet. Later, a bunch of guys told Turner I'd kicked it over to him." Justin was hunched forward, his hands laced between the spread of his knees. "He'd had it in for me because he liked Tess too. He thought I'd kicked the paper to him to get him in trouble, on account of how he was always making passes at Tess. But I hadn't. It was just his luck it landed there."

"Did he get kicked out of school?"

"No. He got a zero for the grading period."

"And Tess didn't 'fess up?"

Justin gave me a look of disbelief. "You've got to be kidding."

"So you broke Turner's arm for messing with your girl."

His eyes squinted with cynicism. "Right!" I could tell this was still a sore matter for him. "Turner came after me the next day and punched me. We started to whop each other and I wrestled him to the ground. His buddies rallied around us and shouted. At one point, I pinned him to the ground, a knee on his chest and the other on his arm. I didn't realize there was a tree root above ground under his arm. When I laid my weight on it, I heard an awful muffled crack." Justin smiled sadly. "Turner yowled. His arm was bent at a weird angle. Talk about geometry!"

"Ugh!"

"So, they kicked me out. That's it." Justin glanced at me for a reaction. I returned the look, my mouth half-open. "Now do you see that it had nothing to do with bad grades, or my parents falling on hard times, or any other stuff you thought?"

I nodded.

"I just don't like to talk about it. The whole thing was pretty rough. My dad took it pretty seriously."

"I can understand that. So, what's with the bump on your face?" As though it had a will of its own, my hand went to the swelling on his eyebrow. I touched it lightly with the tips of my fingers.

"Ouch!" Justin pulled back slightly, but a smile washed over his face.

"I'm sorry."

He took my hand in his. "Turner went looking for me the other night."

"I guess he found you." I chuckled. "Is the grudge over with now?"

"I hope so." I was glad Justin could laugh at his situation. "He's dating Tess and this makes him think he got even with me."

"Does it bother you?" My voice drifted into a tentative whisper. "Do you still care about her?"

"After everything she put me through?" His eyebrow arched. "I'm glad he's got her. He deserves her!"

Justin was looking at me in a way that made me feel he could stare into my naked soul. My breathing became fast and uneven. Before I realized what was happening, he covered my frozen smile with his lips, kissing me tenderly and stirring a swell of sensations in me.

"I don't care about Tess anymore," he whispered close to my lips. "I care about you."

A surge of electricity made me tremble inside. No one had ever laid out his true feelings for me before.

Justin pulled me to him and pressed his lips on mine. His mouth gave, yet demanded. A wave of warm pleasant feelings coursed through me. His hair felt soft, where my fingers landed on the back of his head. I had no recollection of reaching up to him. I was annoyed at myself. Something inside me resisted. Zach and I would be having dinner at his house in a few days. Who was to say what route our friendship would take? I shouldn't be playing games with Justin. I shouldn't mislead him. Justin was a nice guy.

I pushed against his chest gently. "Don't."

He loosened his hold, but didn't release me. "What's going on?"

I hesitated for a moment. "It just isn't right."

"You had a good time tonight, didn't you?" Justin asked, looking into my eyes.

"Just because we had fun together doesn't mean I have to repay you by kissing." I was afraid I'd said it too harshly. The moment the words left my mouth, little lines appeared on his forehead.

"Of course not." He let go of me. "I didn't mean it that way."

Neither of us said a word for a few moments. Though the silence lasted only seconds, it felt thick and heavy.

He spoke first. "Is there someone else?"

I nodded, looking down. "Something like that." I ached inside, knowing I'd hurt his feelings. Justin bit his lip. "Besides, I think I should get Susie out of the room before it's too late."

Justin got up. "Don't worry. Carlos will have to come out and empty his wallet now. The pizza man is here."

"I didn't hear the doorbell."

"Believe me, I did."

From his tone, I could tell Justin was glad to have an excuse to end our terrible moment. I watched him lope back in the house, his shoulders rounded.

Susie, Carlos and Justin brought out pizza and drinks to the table by the pool. I thought it was strange to see Carlos pull up a chair by Justin, when there was an empty seat next to Susie. His eyebrows were knitted. She didn't have much to say, and I noticed she'd toned down her flirting. I couldn't eat but one slice of pizza; there was a knot in my stomach.

Somehow, the evening had soured. No one cracked jokes or laughed as we'd done earlier. Susie asked the boys to take us home right after we ate.

I was confused. Though Justin had respected my wishes, I felt an odd sense of loss, like I'd somehow cheated myself and ended up the loser at this game.

Chapter 8

I didn't hear from Susie for a few days, and I didn't bother to call her. I was still stinging from her attitude towards me at Justin's house. I decided to call her the day after Christmas to give her my present. I was sure she'd be curious about my day at Zach's.

Mami and I went to Misa de Gallo, the midnight mass on Christmas Eve named after the roosters whose morning crowing began as the mass let out. In spite of our late bedtime, I managed to get up before seven on Christmas morning so that we could enjoy time together before she left for work. Mami scrambled eggs with chorizo, my favorite Spanish sausage, and I warmed up the milk for cocoa. We opened presents and had our traditional breakfast in the living room by the elaborate Nacimiento, with its tiny ceramic statues of the Holy Family, the three wise men, shepherds and countless animals witnessing Jesus' birth. Every year we added special ceramic pieces to it. Mami and I set up the figures on a miniature landscape of boxes covered with sheets of crumpled brown and olive green paper. Over the years, the Nacimiento had expanded so that now it rambled over a grouping of side and coffee tables and cascaded down to floor level. It was the centerpiece of the season's decorations.

As I had hoped, Abuela sent me the running shoes I wanted. She also inserted a ten-dollar bill into each shoe to spend on anything I pleased when I wore the shoes. I ran to the phone to thank her, forgetting how early it would be in Chicago because of the difference in time zones. Abuela said she didn't mind the early hour. She said that for me, she'd wake up anytime.

Our celebration was short, but this year I was so excited about having Christmas dinner with Zach that I didn't complain about Mami's work schedule.

After she left, I showered and worked on my hair until every strand was smooth and perfectly in place. I selected a cotton sweater from the presents Mami had given me. It was royal blue, a shade that brought out the pink in my cheeks, and also went well with my new black pants. I wore silver earrings, one a stick figure of a girl, the other a boy, and a matching bracelet that alternated boys and girls holding hands. Among all my presents, these had been my favorite.

I was ready ahead of time, but I didn't want to hang around on the front porch and appear anxious. So, I stepped out for a jasmine and returned to the living room to wait. Mrs. Maxwell would have Zach pick me up as soon as he arrived at her house. I let the plucked petals of the jasmine tumble onto my pants. I didn't care about the mess. The last petal said he loved me, and that was all I cared about. As I brought it to my lips to kiss it for luck, Zach tapped the Blazer's horn three times.

I ran to the door, slipping on the wood floor in my new chunky-heeled moccasins. "I'll be right out," I shouted through the crack of the door.

Zach was coming up the steps of the porch, while the Blazer idled in the driveway.

"Merry Christmas!" I said.

"Yeah. Merry Christmas!" He stepped into the house behind me.

"I just have to grab a few things," I told him, tossing my black purse over my shoulder and rushing into the kitchen.

"Would you believe Grams made me come in to get you? She said it was rude to blow the horn."

"Everybody does it. I'm used to it," I was trying to sound casual but I was mortified. Mami had baked ripe plantains for me to take to Mrs. Sherwood. She said it wasn't necessary to buy my hosts presents, especially since I had never met Zach's parents. But a gift of food was the right thing and could be enjoyed by the whole family, Mami had said. The dish went well with ham, turkey or pork and they were bound to have one of those as the main course. I dreaded to see their reaction to a Cuban dish at an American Christmas party.

"Geez! This is the biggest manger scene I've ever seen!" I heard him exclaim.

"The Nativity?" I carried the warm casserole wrapped in clean dish towels into the living room.

"The darn thing takes up a third of the room!" He scratched the blond cowlick at the crown of his head. "It must take you hours to put it together!"

"We love setting it up. The landscape turns out a different way every year." The ceramic angel blowing the trumpet over the stable had slipped on his side. I made a mental note to straighten it when I got back. "Every time we unwrap a figure, it's like making a discovery."

"Is this a Cuban thing? Making such a big production of this?"

"I never thought of it," I answered, examining the scene in a new light, as if seeing it through someone else's eyes. "I guess it's a Cuban tradition. Every Cuban family I know sets one up."

"Do they put this much work into it?"

"Sure. After all, the birth of Jesus is what Christmas is all about."

"Where's your tree?"

"Over there." I thrust my chin in the direction of the family room.

He eyed the tree with surprise. I was sure he thought it was strange that the tree had a secondary role in our home.

"Can you bring that present on the couch? It's for your grandma. And grab my keys and lock the door, please."

Seeing that I was balancing the dish with caution, Zach opened the front passenger door for me.

"Merry Christmas, Maggie," Mrs. Maxwell piped up from the back seat. "You look beautiful in that shade of blue."

"Thank you." I was annoyed at the rush of warmth that flushed over my face. I didn't dare look in Zach's direction. "What are you doing in the back seat? You should be sitting up front."

"No, no. The front seat is for the young people. Besides, I've got to hold on to all these presents I'm bringing."

Mrs. Maxwell was surrounded by packages in colorful wrappings and ribbons. Her forest green suit showed off her creamy skin and her halo of white curls. Over her heart, she had pinned a lacquered brooch in the shape of a red poinsettia.

"Well, Grams, here's one more," Zach said, as he slid into his seat and handed her my present. "It's from Maggie to you."

For a moment, Mrs. Maxwell looked confused. My ears and face warmed up with added embarrassment. Zach left the package in his grandmother's hands and started the engine.

"Zachary! Where's your courtesy?" Mrs. Maxwell gasped. "If it's Maggie's present, then it's not your place to hand it to me!"

Zach stole a smirking glance at me. "Oops!" he said.

"Don't mind him, Maggie. When we open presents, I'll know this one is from you." Mrs. Maxwell sighed deeply and, though I didn't turn around to look at her, I could picture her wagging her head of white curls. "If it wasn't so hard to get in and out of this truck, I'd move to the front seat to keep you in line, young man."

Zach chuckled. "Oh, Grams . . ."

The Sherwood home was a two-story stucco structure with impressive Spanish arches and dark wooden shutters. On the moist and shady sections of its red barrel tile roof, moss and ferns had taken hold. Though built in the early part of the century when the elegant city of Coral Gables was carved out of the rocky hammocks, the house seemed to have been transported from a medieval Spanish village. I'd always wondered how Americans found the architecture of my ancestors so appealing while often disliking the ways of their descendants.

Enormous live oaks flanked the corners of the house, cooling the front yard with their protective shade. Where the sun-loving St. Augustine grass was sparse, English ivy rambled over the ground and wound around the gnarled trunks. Masses of pink, purple and white impatiens lined the stone path and edged the foot of the foundation plantings. A pair of twig deer, wearing plaid bows at their necks, decorated the lawn for the season. Though resembling a Southern woodland, the wild nature of the landscape had been carefully studied and planned by someone.

A girl, whose age I pinned at thirteen and whom I guessed to be Jennifer from Mrs. Maxwell's descriptions, came out the door. Her straight blond hair bounced on her shoulders as she hurried to the driveway. A younger, tow-headed boy rushed past her yelling, "They're here! Grams is here!"

"Brian! Come give Grandma a hug!" Mrs. Maxwell said, standing by the car door. The boy reached up and smacked her on the cheek.

"Merry Christmas, Grandma," said Jennifer.

"Merry Christmas, sweetie," Mrs. Maxwell said, planting a kiss on her cheek. "I want you to meet Maggie." She put her arm around my shoulder. "This is my granddaughter Jennifer. I think you girls will get along just fine."

"Hi, I'm Brian." The boy had slipped into the back seat and was holding an armful of presents.

"Oh, yes. This is the youngest member of the family." Mrs. Maxwell grinned, a warning pointer wagging at his perky face. "Take those presents in the house, but don't open any until I'm with you."

As I watched Brian heading back to the house, I saw that Mr. and Mrs. Sherwood were now coming down the path. Mr. Sherwood's dark blond hairline was sprinkled with gray, though his tall frame had the athletic strength of a younger man. Mrs. Sherwood had ageless beauty: her figure slim, her hair a natural blond, her manner gracious. I could see where Zach had gotten his good looks. After exchanging hugs with Mrs. Maxwell, Mrs. Sherwood turned to me.

"I'm glad you came, Maggie."

I was somewhat flustered because I couldn't offer a handshake. The warm casserole was still in my hands. "Thank you. My mother made me bring . . .Oh! What I mean is, she made a Cuban dish for your Christmas dinner."

"How wonderful!" Mrs. Sherwood's eyes didn't crinkle like her mother's when she smiled.

"You remembered," Mrs. Maxwell exclaimed. She turned to her daughter and son-in-law. "I asked Maggie for more Cuban food. What she brought me at Thanksgiving was so delicious."

"What is it?" Jennifer asked.

I braced myself for the looks on their faces. "Baked sweet plantains."

"I've had that at a fancy Cuban restaurant. I think you'll love it," Mr. Sherwood said to his family as I breathed a sigh of relief. "Zach, take the dish and put it in the kitchen."

"I'm bringing in the presents," Brian shouted as he zoomed past us with another armful.

As Mrs. Maxwell, her daughter and I started down the stone path to the house, Mr. Sherwood and Jennifer took out the rest of the presents in the truck and shut the door.

"Your house is beautiful!" I said.

"Thank you. We're proud of it," Mrs. Sherwood answered.

"It dates back to the 1920s. It's as old as me." Mrs. Maxwell winked a clear blue eye at me.

"Come on, Mom," Mrs. Sherwood said.

"I guess you love gardening as much as we do," I said to the younger woman. "It must be a lot of work keeping your plants so healthy and beautiful."

Mrs. Maxwell's laugh was fresh. "Oh, dear, no! She doesn't set foot in the yard. The landscapers do all the work."

Mrs. Sherwood gave her mother a gracious smile, but I detected a touch of irritation behind it. "Be fair, Mom."

"She's right," Mrs. Maxwell said to me. "She has little time left after all her civic meetings and fund raisers and looking after the house and the kids."

"And you!" Mrs. Sherwood added.

"Just teasing, darling. You're a wonderful daughter. Between you and Maggie, I'm very well cared for."

"There's still the matter of getting your house cleaned, Mom. You're in no condition to be doing it yourself. You know that's what I expected from the arrangement." Her voice trailed off into a whisper, as though the comment was meant only for her mother's ears.

My mouth went dry. It seemed Mrs. Sherwood had only wanted me as a maid for her mother.

"Now dear, Christmas is not the time to nag." Mrs. Maxwell put an arm around my shoulder and drew me to her. "Besides, I've brought a guest that I'd like you make welcome in your home."

Mrs. Sherwood stepped aside for her mother and me to enter the foyer. The home was impeccably decorated in fashionable plaids and flowered prints, in sunny yellows, peach and green. Though the furniture was new, its style was in keeping with the age of the house, if not its Spanish lines. The sound of Christmas carols grew more distinct as we passed the formal living room. I moved along with the group to the family room, which opened to a large modern kitchen and on the opposite side had a wall of windows to the swimming pool and patio. The tallest Christmas tree I'd ever seen inside a house stood at the end of the room, and its base was now surrounded by the packages Brian had brought in from the truck. I scanned the room for a Nativity, but there was none.

"Let's open the presents you brought, Grams!" Brian pleaded.

Mrs. Sherwood slipped into the kitchen. "Not until we've had dinner."

"But I can't wait that long to see what Grams got for me," Brian moaned.

"You'd think you didn't get any presents this morning," said Mr. Sherwood.

"What's the big deal? Why should feather-brain have to wait until he eats?" Zach snapped.

Mrs. Sherwood gave him a warning glance. "Zach, be nice."

"We're not just eating, Zach," his father said. "We're having Christmas dinner. That's a big deal."

Jennifer brought glasses of iced soda for me and her grandmother. She changed the CD from choir hymns to lively carols, then sat on the couch next to me.

"Just one present, Grams?" Brian held up a box and gave his grandmother a look worthy of Tiny Tim.

"Let the boy open his presents," Mrs. Maxwell said, handing me a cracker that she'd lathered with salmon spread. She whispered, "Eat, dear. Don't be shy."

Mrs. Sherwood put a dish of freshly baked finger food on the counter that separated the kitchen from the family room and, without a word, Jennifer transferred it to the coffee table. The flaky pastries were topped with colorful dollops of green (which I guessed to be spinach), red (probably chopped tomatoes), and a cheese and sausage mixture. Though the aroma of baked cheese and onions was teasing my appetite, I waited for Mrs. Maxwell to place one of each on a little glass plate for me. I smiled gratefully, taking it and a cocktail napkin from her hands.

From the kitchen side of the counter, Mrs. Sherwood gave her youngest child a nod of approval. "Okay. You can open all your presents before dinner."

"Yes!" Brian screeched, tearing the paper from the box he'd picked.

"Take it easy, son. Don't tear up what's inside too," Mr. Sherwood advised him.

"It's the latest set of Inter-galactic Reptomorphs," Brian shouted, jumping up and down. "I needed these to complete my collection! Thank you, Grams."

"Let me see that, you kangamorph!" Zach snatched the box from the boy.

"Give it back!"

It seemed Zach had a knack for chafing his little brother with funny names and teasing. I wasn't sure I liked that. He had the advantage of age and size over Brian. For some reason, I realized I'd never heard Justin call others names. Then again, he didn't have the aggravation of little brothers and sisters.

Zach took out a couple of the plastic reptilian-looking creatures and pretended to speak for them. "Argh! We'll eat the kangamorph when it gets dark. Wroof! We'll come to life when the quasi-human is alone in his room."

In spite of his anger, Brian laughed. Jennifer and I joined in.

"Don't worry, Brian," Mrs. Maxwell assured the boy. "Plastic figures can't come to life. I don't want you to be scared later."

"I know that, Grams. Zach can't scare me."

"Yeah, right. Wait 'til Mom and Dad go out one night and leave me in charge. I'll turn into a spiny specter."

A picture of Justin and I stepping into the dark water raced through my mind. Instead of adding to my fears that night, Justin had reassured me. I wondered if Zach would have done the same.

"You're *already* one, Zach," Mr. Sherwood told him.

"He's just showing off, Dad," Brian said. "He's being cute for Maggie."

Jennifer broke out in giggles and once more, I felt the heat travel to my cheeks.

"Maggie's just a friend, bronto-breath." Zach handed back the box to Brian and searched under the tree for presents. "Here's one for Miss Pretty Prissy," he said, handing a box to his sister, who rewarded him with an ugly grimace as she took it from his hands. "One for Grams; one for Maggie . . ."

"For me?" I asked shyly. I was troubled about not having gifts for the Sherwood family. I hoped Mami was right about bringing food instead.

"Jennifer helped me find the right gift for you." Mrs. Sherwood added milk to the mashed potatoes in the mixer. "I hope you like it."

After emptying out bundles of colored tissue paper from the large decorated gift bag, I brought out a black denim jacket and a matching skirt. "They're beautiful! Thank you."

Mrs. Maxwell's eyes widened with delight when she saw the present I gave her. "This is a gorgeous throw." She spread open the cotton blanket and admired the pattern of boxes with potted plants in the center of each.

"The colors are rich, Mom," Mrs. Sherwood said, glancing at it from the other side of the counter. "It's perfect for your lap, when you sit in the Florida room to read the morning paper."

"I have a present for you too," Mrs. Maxwell told me. "Zach, would you hand me the small box for Maggie?"

The little package was covered in black and gold metallic wrap, with a tiny gold ribbon and bow. "It's too pretty to open."

Zach laughed. "Oh, no! Another one of those silly girls like my sister, who hates to tear nice paper."

Jennifer leered at him. "Pretend he doesn't exist. He's a spiny specter."

I opened the package carefully, setting aside the precious gold ribbon. The little box snapped open when I pressed a button in the front. Inside the red velvet lined box were pearl earrings with a small ruby on each. "Oh, Mrs. Maxwell, you shouldn't have. This is too nice."

"Nonsense. This is what I want to give you."

"Ooh!" Jennifer leaned closer to peek in the box. "I like them. Look, Mom."

Mrs. Sherwood glanced over the counter at the contents of the box. "Very nice," she said distractedly. "Maggie, do the plantains need to be warmed up? Dinner's almost ready."

"I guess they can go in the microwave for a couple of minutes." I got up and made my way into the kitchen, unsure whether I should be helping with the meal. At home, I usually gave Mami a hand.

"Time for my performance." Getting up from his chair, Mr. Sherwood rubbed his hands together. I thought perhaps he played a musical instrument and it was their tradition for him to play it now. But he joined us in the kitchen, tested the sharpness of the knife and began to carve the turkey.

Jennifer and I helped Mrs. Sherwood take the serving dishes into the dining room. The vegetables were served in bowls that matched the flowered china. Condiments and bread had been placed in various silver servers. I was aware that my casserole wasn't fancy enough for such a dressy table. The dark wood pedestal table was set with sparkling crystal and china, and topped with a centerpiece of gold sprayed pears, apples and nuts and gold ribbons laced in the spaces between the fruit. "Jingle Bells," a song I associated with the cold winters of the north more than with a spiritual Christmas, played in the background.

As I hung back waiting to be assigned a seat, Mrs. Maxwell placed her hand on the backrest of one of the dark carved chairs. "Sit here, Maggie. Right between me and Jennifer."

I noticed that Zach had taken the seat across from me and the skin of my neck prickled as our eyes met.

"Can you pass the smashed potatoes?" he asked me.

"They're mashed, Zach, not smashed!" Jennifer glared at her older brother.

"They look smashed to me." Zach grinned.

Jennifer rolled her eyes to the heavens.

I lifted the dish, which had been placed in front of me, and stretched my arm across the table. The serving dishes traveled around the table as each person took a helping. I scooped up small amounts, not wanting to let them think I was fainting with hunger, though the steamy aroma of onions, green beans and turkey was making my mouth water. At home, I would have heaped my plate with food this good.

Mr. Sherwood raised his glass of white wine. "Here's to health, to a happy family and to our guest."

We raised our stem glasses, though the children's were filled with Sprite instead of wine.

"And to lots of money!" Brian piped in.

"That's a pretty materialistic wish at Christmas, Brian." Mrs. Sherwood set her blue eyes on her youngest child.

"What's that?"

"Greedy. You bronto-brain." Zach snickered. "But I'll have to admit that's a pretty cool wish."

"Zach!" His father gave him a stern look.

Our hands and glasses were still raised.

"Okay, okay," said Mr. Sherwood. "May all our Christmas wishes come to pass."

The room was filled with the clinking of crystal. Then, each person took a sip of his drink. I set down my glass, laced my hands together on my lap and dipped my head. But, instead of a prayer of thanks before the meal, I heard the familiar plinking of silverware as the others sliced the food on their china plates. At home, we always said a prayer before a holiday meal. I peeked through lowered lashes. Everyone at the table had started eating. Hoping no one had noticed my bowed head, I quickly thanked God for all the good things in my life. I didn't make the sign of the cross; I felt too self-conscious. I simply picked up my fork and caught up with the activity at the table.

The first morsel in my mouth was white meat. It was tender, with just the right amount of moisture. I kept my eyes on my plate, too shy to look up across the table at Zach while I chewed.

"Were you able to spend time with your mother this morning?" Mrs. Maxwell asked.

I gave her a series of nods, as my mouth was full at the moment.

She smiled. "I'm glad. I was afraid she'd have to work so early."

"How come she has to work on Christmas?" Brian asked.

"Because she works in a hospital and hospitals have to keep running, even on Christmas," Mrs. Sherwood answered.

"Is she a doctor?" Jennifer asked.

As I was ready to answer, Mrs. Sherwood shook her head and a subtle smile appeared on her lips. "She changes beds and cleans up. Right, Maggie?"

As if zapped by lightning, my body stiffened. My mom wasn't an orderly! She'd worked hard for her nursing degree.

Mrs. Maxwell came to the rescue. "Mrs. Castillo is a nurse. And Maggie's father was a doctor, mind you."

Mrs. Sherwood raised an eyebrow.

"He's not a doctor anymore? Was he kicked out of the hospital or something?" Zach asked.

It was Mrs. Maxwell's turn to blush, though I was sure it was from anger at her grandson's tactless ways rather than embarrassment. "Maggie's father died, Zachary."

Zach pressed his lips together. "I'm sorry. I didn't know."

I accepted his apology with a nod.

"What was his specialty?" Mr. Sherwood asked, interest warming his blue eyes.

"He was going to be a pediatrician, but his illness took hold when he was interning."

"That's a foot doctor, right?" Zach offered.

Mr. Sherwood inhaled. "A foot doctor is a podiatrist. A pedi-atrician works with children."

"I was just kidding." Zach grinned. But he didn't fool me. I figured he'd claimed to be kidding to save face.

"Maggie's mom works in the pediatrics wing of the hospital. She takes care of patients just as Maggie takes care of me," his grandmother said.

"Are you a nurse?" Jennifer asked me, wide eyed.

"I'm gonna be one," I said.

Mrs. Maxwell patted my hand. "As far as I'm concerned, she already is one."

"That's impressive, Maggie," Mr. Sherwood told me, but instead of glancing in my direction, he glared at Zach. "I don't know too many kids your age who know what they want in life."

"Frosty the Snowman" blared from the family room. Mrs. Sherwood broke the uncomfortable silence that followed. "I'm grateful your mother took the time to cook this dish for us. Tell her the plantains are delicious," Mrs. Sherwood said.

"What country is this dish from?" Brian asked.

"Cuba," Mrs. Sherwood offered. "Maggie is Cuban."

I smiled shyly. Though I'd been taught it wasn't polite to correct adults, I couldn't help it this time. "I'm not Cuban. I'm American. I've never been to Cuba. I was born in Miami."

"Well, her parents were born on the island," Mrs. Sherwood told Brian. "that makes her Cuban-American, I suppose."

"The plantains aren't cooked the way I'm used to having them," Mr. Sherwood interrupted, his purposeful tone indicat-ing the previous subject was closed. "I don't think I've had them in a sauce before," said Mr. Sherwood.

I was glad that the plantains had been very ripe, because they'd cooked to sweet perfection. The sauce had thickened to darkest brown from the red wine, brown sugar and cinnamon in it. "That's because restaurants usually fry them," I explained. "When they're baked with red wine and sugar we call the dish 'Temptation.'"

"They are tempting," Mrs. Maxwell said.

"I thought I detected the wine in it." Mr. Sherwood smiled.

"Wine?" Brian perked up. "I'm gonna have some more and see if I get drunk."

"You can't get drunk from gravy, you gobbler!" Zach teased.

"How would you know?" Brian retorted, lifting the lid from the casserole. "You haven't even tried it."

I ventured a glance at Zach's plate. There were neither plantains nor a tell-tale puddle of sauce.

"You never like to try exotic stuff," Jennifer said. "You could be missing out on something good."

"I'm just watching to see if any of you passes out." Zach's lips curled into a mocking grin. "If the food is safe, then I'll try it."

I stared down at my plate.

Brian rested the glass lid on the table and began to select another small piece.

"Brian, don't put the lid on the linen tablecloth. Red wine stains don't come out!" When Mrs. Sherwood lifted the lid, its square edges were outlined in dark sauce on the white tablecloth.

I was sorry to see that the food I brought had been the cause of a problem. "I'll take the tablecloth home. I'm sure my mom knows how to get rid of the stain."

"That won't be necessary, Maggie," Mrs. Sherwood said, turning to set the lid on the buffet behind her. "But thank you anyway."

"I want some more to see if something happens to me." Jennifer laughed. She dripped a spoonful of the sauce on the plantains on her plate.

"Okay," said Zach. "I'll try the stuff. Shovel a little on my plate, Maggie."

By now, the casserole had made its way to me. Zach shoved his plate in at me over the fruit centerpiece. I spooned a portion of plantain, then tried to steady his plate with my other hand, but to my horror, the sauce dribbled from the spoon onto the white tablecloth.

"Zachary!" I heard Mrs. Sherwood exclaim.

But everyone could see that it wasn't his fault. "I'm so sorry," I said.

"It's all right, dear," Mrs. Maxwell said, patting the spots with tissues she'd dug out of her pocket.

"This wouldn't have happened if you kids hadn't been playing games with the food." Mrs. Sherwood dampened a few paper napkins with iced water from her glass and passed them down to her mother. "The alcohol is cooked out of the wine, anyway."

"Hey, you're always telling me to try new foods," Zach snapped at his mother. "Now I get blamed for going for it. I can't win."

"You could have asked her to pass the serving dish," said Mrs. Sherwood.

Brian craned his neck to check the damage, as his grandmother continued to rub the spots. "They won't come out. They're spreading."

"Don't start acting so innocent," Jennifer told her little brother. "You ruined it first."

"That's enough!" Mr. Sherwood stared at his children. "If the tablecloth is ruined, we'll buy another one. What's the big problem?"

"Another Irish linen tablecloth?" Mrs. Sherwood raised her eyebrows at her husband who sat at the head of the table. "Do you know how expensive linen can be?"

I wanted to slide under the table.

Mrs. Maxwell tucked her chin and gave her daughter a meaningful look. "Well, that's the price we pay for raising children. Anyone can have an accident. Right, dear?"

Mrs. Sherwood nodded, but I could detect displeasure through her veil of politeness. "Yes, it was an accident. I didn't mean to make you feel uncomfortable, Maggie."

I was sure my face glowed deep crimson. "I'd like to take it home and see what my mom can do about the stains."

Mrs. Sherwood shook her head but her eyes didn't meet mine as she said, "That's all right. I'll try cleaning it myself."

"Why don't you let Maggie take it home? I'm sure Mrs. Castillo has battled this kind of stain before. Anyway, it will make Maggie feel better," Mrs. Maxwell told her daughter.

Mrs. Sherwood gave in. "Oh, I suppose she can."

Jennifer took me to her room after dinner to show me the clothes she had gotten for Christmas. I was relieved to be away from the adults, as my mood had changed from happy anticipation to deep embarrassment. I think Jennifer was aware of my feelings, because after going over every one of her gifts, she asked me to help her put together outfits for school. That took up the better part of the afternoon. I was grateful.

I was too flustered to be around Zach. For some reason, I didn't mind passing up on a chance to be with him. For days I had dreamed of the special talks Zach and I would have today. I had nursed hope that he'd overcome whatever was holding him back from asking me out. In my mind, I had pictured his room in the same condition as his Bronco, basketballs and books on the floor and his smelly jersey thrown in a corner, and I'd accepted his messy habit as a charming quality. But I hadn't even peeked in his room. And I wasn't sure I wanted to anymore. As for his asking me out, I was beginning to wonder if it was meant to happen after all. But one thing I knew: It wasn't going to happen this Christmas day.

When Zach knocked on the door to tell us Mrs. Maxwell thought it was time to go, I was glad. I thanked Mr. and Mrs. Sherwood for inviting me. Zach gave me a hand carrying to his truck my presents, the casserole and the stained tablecloth, which Mrs. Maxwell had folded and placed in a shopping bag. Jennifer and Brian helped Mrs. Maxwell with her packages. The family stood in the front yard waving as Zach backed the Bronco to take us home.

"I hope you know what you're doing with Mom's tablecloth," he said with a snort as he drove.

Anger roiled in my head.

"It'll be fine," Mrs. Maxwell assured him.

"I'd hate to be around Mom if it doesn't clean up."

"It's only a tablecloth, Zachary. It can be replaced." Mrs. Maxwell reached up from the back seat and patted my shoulder. I wondered if she could feel it sizzle from the angry heat boiling in me. "You and Brian had a part in the spills, Zachary. Don't make it sound as though Maggie was responsible for the stains. She's not. What happened was an accident."

In spite of what she said, I couldn't help thinking that if I hadn't brought the plantains, there wouldn't have been any stains.

"Yeah, Grams!" Zach answered her. "But I'm the one who'll have to put up with Mom's bitching."

"Zachary! Watch your tongue with me, young man!"

Chapter 9

I was glad to be back in the refuge of my home. Glad that I didn't have to smile politely at Mrs. Maxwell, when I really felt so miserable about the stained tablecloth. I was also relieved to be away from Zach's territory.

A friend would have backed me up and made me feel comfortable. Instead, Zach had only looked out for himself. His attitude disappointed me. Besides feeling miserable about the damaged tablecloth, I now felt betrayed. I had counted on his friendship. What's more, I had dared to dream he had deeper feelings for me. A heavy hurt settled in my chest.

I dropped the tablecloth in the laundry room. As I stored the leftover plantains in the refrigerator, I looked for something that I could make for our dinner. It would have to be simple and fast. And it would not include plantains. I never wanted to see baked plantains again. I decided on ham and cheese sandwiches and tomato soup, which was Mami's favorite. Then I straightened out my room, found a place for all my presents, and gathered all the torn gift-wrap from our morning celebration in the living room. I sighed when I found the wilted jasmine petals that I'd plucked while waiting for Zach. I made sure I picked up each one and, with a startling sense of relief, threw them out the front door. The house was spotless and serene.

It was tough enough that Mami had to work on Christmas day. It wouldn't be fair to expect her to work at home also. Besides, I needed her help and I wanted her to be in a good mood when she walked in the door.

"*¡Caramba!*" I heard Mami say, as she removed the key from the lock. "This morning's mess is gone! It must be the magic of Christmas."

I ran up to her and put my arms around her. "I put away all my presents and made dinner, too."

"I should have known. You caught some exotic disease," she said, laughing. She tried to press her palm to my forehead. "Let's see if you're burning up with fever."

I chuckled and wriggled away. "I help you around the house."

"Sure," she answered, her eyes drawn into teasing slits. "On holidays or when you want something from me."

"*¡Ay, Mami!* I'm not like that," I pretended to complain. I followed her to her bedroom and sprawled on her bed as she removed her uniform and changed into cotton knit pants and a sweatshirt.

"How was your day with Mrs. Maxwell's family?"

I made a face of disgust.

"What happened?" The sweatshirt hovered above her head, her arms threaded through the sleeves, as she waited for my answer.

"Everything went wrong. I was so embarrassed!"

She slipped the shirt over her head.

"The sauce from the baked plantains spilled on Mrs. Sherwood's tablecloth. It's got a bunch of stains."

"*¡Ay, Dios mío!* That's terrible." She grabbed my hand and pulled me up. "Let's eat. I'm very hungry. So, what else went wrong?"

"Well, that was it," I said, following her to the kitchen. "I feel terrible about it."

"You said everything went wrong." Mami stirred the soup.

"That was bad enough. Don't you think?" I avoided mentioning my disappointment in Zach.

"Sure it was, *mi vida.*" Her hand felt warm on my cheek. "But it's not the end of the world. Mrs. Sherwood will get the stain out."

"Well," I said, unable to look her in the eye. "I told her you'd know what to do. I figured you had cleaned up this type of sauce before."

"I've never spilled it on anything nice. What kind of fabric is it?"

"Linen."

"Uh-oh. Sounds like a delicate, expensive tablecloth. No wonder you felt badly about it." She put our plates, with sandwiches and olives, on the table. "Call her and tell her to treat the spots overnight with a stain removing detergent. Hopefully, that will do it."

I bit my lip. "I can't tell her that. Mrs. Sherwood doesn't have the tablecloth."

"She sent it to the cleaners?" Mami glanced at me. I knew where her thoughts were leading when she raised one eyebrow. "The cleaners are closed on Christmas day, aren't they?"

I made my eyebrows scrunch and my bottom lip pout, like a pitiful ragamuffin, and then bobbed my head slowly.

"Did her mother take it home with her?"

I shook my head even more gently.

Mami stared at me for a moment, then stepped into the laundry room. "Maggie," she said with dismay, unfolding the white lace cloth. "I can't believe you expect me to take out the stains. You've put me in a tough situation."

"What else could I do, Mami? If it wasn't for the dish I brought, this wouldn't have happened."

Mami inspected the dark spatters closely. After a moment, she reached for the creamy concentrated detergent she used on grimy spots. She rubbed it on the damaged areas of the table-cloth. "Let it stand like this overnight. Put it in the washer in the morning, then we'll see if it worked."

"And if the stains are still there . . .?"

"There's nothing we can do." Mami shrugged sadly.

"What about bleach? We could put some in the wash."

Mami looked at me wide-eyed. "I wouldn't try that."

"Why not?"

"It could break down the fibers. That happened to me once with a cotton uniform that I'd spilled *picadillo* on. When I scrubbed the spot with a squirt of bleach, it ate up the fabric and worked a hole in it." She cocked her head and pressed her lips. "Besides, this tablecloth is a delicate piece."

"I know." I was disappointed. I had counted on Mami having all the answers.

Mami put her arm around me and walked me back to the kitchen. "Let's eat our dinner and enjoy what's left of the day. We'll see what happens tomorrow."

As I served the soup into two bowls, Mami reached in the refrigerator for drinks. "You brought back the leftover plantains. Wonderful!"

The hairs on my neck stood up. I didn't even want to *smell* the plantains again.

"I'll put them in the microwave and we'll have them with the ham sandwiches."

I was glad I had my back to her and she couldn't see the disgust that washed over my face. "They don't really go with soup and sandwiches."

I heard her chuckle proudly. "My plantains go with everything."

Mami planted a kiss on my cheek as she left for work the next morning. "Don't waste the day in bed, sleepyhead."

"Hrmph!" was my half-conscious answer.

"I put the tablecloth in the washer."

"Thanks," I grunted.

"I hope you keep the house as neat as you had it yesterday."

I rolled over, pulling the covers over my head.

"Call me at work and let me know how the tablecloth comes out. See, you later."

"*Adiós, Mami,*" I whispered, barely moving my lips.

I had no recollection of hearing another sound that morning, until a loud clattering at my window sprang me from a deep sleep. I sat up in bed trying to make sense of my surroundings.

"Maggie, wake up! I know you're in there!" I heard Susie yelling. Then, I heard more clattering. She was banging on my bedroom window with her knuckles. "I need to talk to you."

I parted the slats of the blinds. Susie stood in the glare of the sun holding a gift-wrapped package. I tapped on the glass. "Come around to the front door."

I shaded my eyes from the bright light and let her in. "Why didn't you call and tell me you were coming?"

She looked at me sheepishly. "I didn't know if you were mad at me. You know, from the way I acted when we were at Justin's . . ."

I shrugged my shoulders. I had been a little miffed.

Susie followed me into my bedroom. "You haven't called me the last few days. I didn't know what to think."

I flung a side glance at her, while searching for a pair of jeans in a drawer. "Is your dialing finger in a cast? You haven't called me either."

She lowered her eyes. "I know. I was too crushed and embarrassed."

"Why? What happened?" I kicked the drawer shut and slipped into my jeans.

"Oh, Maggie. It was terrible! You were right."

Goose pimples crawled over my skin. "Oh, no! You didn't!"

"No, I didn't. Carlos wanted to, you know, when you left us in Justin's bedroom. But I said no."

"Oh, Suze," I said, reaching for her hand.

"Please, don't call me that. That was his name for me."

I gave her a sympathetic smile.

"He told me what he wanted. When I said no, he said it was over between us." She plopped down on my bed.

"No wonder neither of you looked happy while we ate the pizza." Things fell into place. Susie had asked to be taken home right after that. "I bet you feel hurt."

"I cried for three days. Mamá wanted to know why I was so sad. I couldn't tell her the truth. So I finally said you and I had argued."

"You rat!" I aimed an accusatory finger at her. "Putting the blame on me!"

"What are friends for? She was really happy to drive me over when I told her I wanted to make up."

"You should have called me sooner. You know we can always talk."

"I felt too stupid. You warned me about Carlos. I guess I was blinded by my feelings. I couldn't see what you pointed out."

I thought about Zach. Susie had told me I'd been reeling in the wrong fishing line. Zach hadn't taken my hook. But I'd been determined to give him every opportunity to show me he did care. I made a big thing of every little word he shared with me, I perceived feelings that weren't there, and I overlooked what I didn't want to accept. The other reel—one that I didn't even know I'd baited—was spinning and whirling. Susie had even pointed it out. I'd also been blind and deaf to that.

I smiled shyly. "I guess we see only what we choose to see, when we think we're in love."

Susie nodded. "I brought your Christmas present." She pushed the box toward me.

I slipped my finger under the wrap, loosening the tape, then worked the bright paper off. In the box was a pair of denim overalls we had both checked out when we went shopping together. "I love them! This is what I wanted. How did you know?"

"Because you told me at the store, silly." Susie winked her eye. "Besides I loved them too."

"I noticed." I got on all fours and reached under my bed. "Here's what I got for you."

A bubble of anticipation expanded in my chest. It burst into a cascade of giggles as she lifted the lid off her box.

"I can't believe it!" Her eyes grew wide and her mouth broke into a grin. "You got me the same overalls."

"I could tell that's what you wanted." I held my pants by the straps and dangled them in front of me. "I had to get them for you."

Susie held up her present the way you'd hang clothes on a paper doll. We stared in the mirror. "We look like twins," she said.

"We should," I agreed. "We even think alike."

We both laughed.

"So tell me about your day with Zach."

I made a grimace of disgust. "It was terrible." I told her step by step everything that happened at Zach's, pausing only to move into the kitchen for some breakfast.

"So, how do you feel about him now?" Susie asked, dunking a piece of my Cuban toast into her *café con leche*.

"I guess I was pretty blind too," I admitted. "I don't think he's so nice anymore."

Susie nodded in silence. I was glad that she didn't rub in her previous warning. I was glad she was a real friend.

She eyed me closely. "Justin's nice."

Her words zapped me like a jolt of electricity. My eyes opened wide. I nodded, unwilling to speak and give away my consternation.

"Has he called you?"

"Nope." I examined the crumbs on my plate.

"He will soon, I'm sure. He really likes you."

I pursed my lips. "I know."

Susie sat on the edge of her chair, leaning close to me, as though fearful she'd miss my answers. "Did he tell you so?"

"Yep!" I said, stirring the dregs of soggy bread crumbs in the bottom of my cup.

"Well? Tell me what happened."

"*Nada*. Nothing happened, Susie."

"Did he kiss you?"

"Susie!" I chuckled nervously. "Give me a break!"

"Yeah, I bet he did. I guess that's when the pizza arrived." I lowered my eyes when she attempted to bore into them with her gaze. "So how come he hasn't called you again?"

"He's not going to call me, Susie. I told him I was interested in someone else."

"*¡Qué loca!* You're nuts! Justin's so cute. I can't believe you let him slip by."

I picked up the breakfast dishes and put them in the dishwasher. I didn't want to tell her that, to my surprise, I did feel some pangs of regret.

"I've got to work on the tablecloth. Come check it out with me." I walked into the laundry room with Susie trailing behind me. "I hope the stains are gone."

Susie helped me pull it out of the washer and spread it out so we could inspect it. "Oh, boy," she said. "I can see them."

"They're lighter than before," I assured her. "But, you're right. What am I gonna do? Mami said if this didn't do it, the stains were there to stay."

"We can try washing it again," she suggested, watching me for an answer.

I shook my head.

"Then let's put a few drops of bleach on the spots."

"No way! I don't want to ruin it." I started to gather the cloth to put it in the dryer.

"Maggie, it *is* ruined." Susie took it from me and set it on top of the washer, spreading the soiled areas flat. "What have you got to lose now? You might as well try it."

"I want to be able to return it in one piece. Mami said bleach could eat up the fibers and make holes in the cloth."

"Not if we dilute the bleach with water. We'll sprinkle it on the stains and rinse the fabric right away. Hand me a cup."

I got a mug from the kitchen, pleased to have someone to help me, yet fearful of the way she was taking over. "Have you done this before?"

"Sure!" Susie poured about a quarter cup of bleach into the mug, then filled it to the top with water. "It'll be an experiment, just like we do in science class."

The smile on her face gave me little reassurance. "*¡Loca!* You're crazy! You haven't tried this before!" I reached for her hand. "Hand me back the mug!"

Susie elbowed me out of the way. "Calm down, *chica*. I've watched Mamá do this many times." She dipped her fingers into the mixture and swabbed the spots with the tips, her hand a pliable brush.

For a moment, I held my breath. Then, with my finger, I tentatively touched the area she had worked on. "The fabric's getting hot, Susie! What does that mean?"

"It's a chemical reaction," she answered confidently. "The bleach's eating up the stains."

"No, it's not! It's eating up the fabric. We're gonna get holes in it!" I grabbed the tablecloth and ran to the kitchen sink. "Quick! We've gotta rinse it off!"

I ran cold water over the treated area until it no longer gave off a strong smell of bleach. I raised it to my nose for a final check. To my amazement, I could no longer find the place where the stain had been. "It worked!" I hopped around the kitchen, yelling excitedly. "¡Mira! Look! The stain's gone!"

Susie shoved past me to inspect the results. She gave me a smug smile. "I told you I'd take it out."

We tried the same procedure on the other stains, my heart racing every time until she allowed me to run water over each spot. Like magic, all the dark stains disappeared. Finally, we ran the tablecloth through a gentle cycle of the wash, to make sure all traces of bleach were rinsed away.

"Oh, I can't believe you did it. You got it clean." I hugged Susie happily. "I've got to call Mami and tell her."

I dialed the pediatric nurses' station at the hospital and, after a few minutes, Mami came on the phone. "I hope this is important, Maggie."

"It is! You'll never guess!"

"Mi vida, I'm busy with patients. I don't have time to guess. What's going on?"

"Susie came over and helped me get the stains out. The tablecloth looks like new!"

"¡Magnífico! I'm glad that special detergent did the job."

"Well, we had to work at them a little more, you know, rub the spots and stuff."

Mami took a deep breath. "You didn't use bleach on the linen, did you?"

I couldn't lie to her. Instead, I avoided the question. "Oh, Susie says 'Hi!'"

Susie tossed me an astonished side glance and smiled.

"I'm glad you're not home by yourself. Tell her 'hello' for me," Mami said. "Listen, mi vida. I've got to get back to work."

"I know. I just wanted to share the good news."

"It's great news. I'll help you iron it and you can take it to Mrs. Maxwell. I bet she'll be pleased when she sees it. I'll talk to you later. Bye."

"See you tonight, Mami."

"Oh, make sure to make a good lunch for yourself and for Susie," she added.

"Don't worry. We'll eat when we're hungry."

"Your mom is just like mine," Susie said, as I hung up the phone. "Always making sure we get enough to eat."

"What else can you expect from a Cuban mom?" I asked her.

"Was she glad to hear about the stains?"

"She thought it was great news. She says she's going to help me iron it so I can take it to Mrs. Maxwell."

"When do you go to her house?"

"Today. I check on her every day during Christmas vacation. Zach's mom can pick up the tablecloth there, next time she visits."

Susie's forehead wrinkled. "Well, that's not what I'd do, if I were you. I wouldn't take it to Mrs. Maxwell." She gave me a devilish smile. "I would hand it to Zach on the first day back to school."

A slow smile worked its way across my face. "Yes! That's it! Zach gave me a hard time about it. He almost challenged me. Now, I can get back at him."

"Then, your heart will be rid of him forever!" Susie exclaimed.

"And the jasmine will never again trick me." As soon as I said it, I realized I'd never told Susie about my habit of relying on the jasmine. I held my breath, afraid she'd make fun of me.

"The what?" Susie stared at me, puzzled.

"I never told you?" I asked innocently.

"I have no idea what you're talking about."

The word was out. I shrugged off my concern. "Come on I'll show you." I grabbed her arm and we ran to the front porch, where the jasmine vine climbed up the wrought iron railing. Its glossy, oval leaves grew a healthy bright green. Scattered among them, were the tiny, fragrant blossoms that I had allowed to mislead me. "Smell the flowers."

Susie leaned into the plant and poked her nose among the white flowers. "Oh, they smell wonderful. It's like perfume."

"You see, every morning before I left for school, I took a flower and plucked the petals one at a time to figure out if Zach loved me. On the days the last petal said he loved me not, bad things would happen. But usually, the last petal said he loved me, and the day would be great. He paid attention to me and good things happened. So I started to rely on the jasmine."

"Wow! I wish you'd told me about this."

I shrugged my shoulders. "I guess I felt it was too silly."

Susie took a flower from the vine and brought it to her nose. "Uhm . . . Lovely." Then, she pulled each petal off, calling out in turn, "He loves me. He loves me not."

The tiny rose-shaped blossom became smaller and smaller, until only the last petal was attached to the stem.

"He loves me not," she called out sadly, as she plucked the last one. She was quiet for a moment. Then, she finally spoke again. "I think the jasmine's telling me the truth. Maybe it is magic."

"Well, if it is, let's make the magic work for us."

"What do you plan to do?" Susie looked up expectantly.

146

"We'll have a ceremony to get Carlos and Zach out of our systems. We'll call it the 'Jasmine Riddance Ritual.' Get it? Rid-*dance*?"

"Pretty clever! I like the idea," Susie said, giggling. She broke off two flowers. "Here's a jasmine for you and one for me."

I held my jasmine in one hand and plucked one petal. "I love him." Then concentrating on my foolish feelings for Zach, I ripped the remaining petals all at once and threw them on the tile of the front porch. "I love him not!" Susie watched me, fascinated. With the grace of a flamenco dancer, I stomped on the remains of the blossom. I sang a loud mourning sound and clapped my hands over my head.

Susie got caught in the mesmerizing rhythm. She followed the same ritual with her blossom and joined me in a lively Spanish dance. We twirled and clapped. We stomped the heels of our boots and sneakers. Our hips swayed. We gathered the sides of invisible flowing skirts and fanned them. We snapped our fingers. We closed our eyes and our voices joined in a loud "*¡Ay, Ay, Ay!*"

"*¡Olé! ¡Olé!*" An old man's voice broke through our song.

I opened my eyes to see Don Vicente, our neighbor across the street clapping and showing off a toothless grin from his front porch. Our song was interrupted as an uncontrollable burst of giggles overtook us. We fell into each other's arms and buried our abashed, laughing faces into the other's shoulder. But only for a moment.

Susie squirmed free and, fired up by the interest of a few older Cuban neighbors who had stepped out to watch, she took up the dance with even more vigor. Though my cheeks still burned with embarrassment, I wasn't going to be left behind. I snapped my fingers, one arm over my head, the other at waist level. I peeked alluringly over my shoulder and hammered out the beat with my boots. The old people clapped to the intense rhythm. With their encouragement, our movements became feverish. Susie and I whirled and stomped and laughed until we collapsed onto the wrought-iron bench on the porch.

Our audience clapped and waved, then retreated back into their homes.

"We're rid of the boys!" Susie yelled victoriously.

"Yes! We're free again!"

Chapter 10

Every time I visited Mrs. Maxwell during Christmas vacation I worried about running into Zach. I didn't want to deal with him until I could put the clean tablecloth in his hands. I was looking forward to seeing the cocky grin on his face turn to amazement when he learned I had dealt with the problem.

I held back from telling Mrs. Maxwell I'd gotten the stains out. I was sorry to have to keep the good news from her, but she'd want me to return the tablecloth to her instead of Zach. I didn't want to miss the opportunity to show him I'd come through the test. Mrs. Maxwell didn't bring up the subject. She probably thought I hadn't had any luck cleaning it. I figured she didn't want to pressure or embarrass me.

I found myself thinking about Justin a few times during the school break. A rush of warm feelings washed over me every time I remembered what he'd said. He had dared to share his feelings for me. I had shut him down. I realized I'd nurtured a senseless hope that he'd call me over the holidays. But he'd be a fool to do so. I had given him no hope for our friendship.

I spent New Year's Eve at Susie's house. We planned the outfits we'd wear on the first day back to school. Susie wanted us to show up in our matching overalls. But I talked her out of it. I had so many new clothes, the decision was hard to make. Since my goal for the first day back was to set Zach straight, we both agreed that the black denim skirt and jacket his family gave me would work to my advantage. It made me feel stylish, yet powerful.

Susie and I had stocked her room with every kind of chip and dip we could find at the store where she worked. We also bought sodas, brownies, cup cakes, cookies and peanuts. By the time midnight came around, we had loaded up on so much junk, we were rubbing our bellyaches.

Mr. Domínguez insisted we join the rest of the family to watch the ball drop at Times Square. Red grapes were portioned to each person in the room. Susie and I exchanged looks of misery as we were handed our dozen grapes. It was going to be a feat to eat the required grapes that would ensure good luck in the new year. As the countdown to midnight began, everyone in the room popped grapes in his mouth, one at a time, until all twelve were gone.

I chewed and swallowed, expecting my stomach to burst with each additional fruit. The juice and the chewed peels traveled a torturous path down my throat. I avoided watching Susie, who was having an even harder time of it than I. Finally, she escaped to the bathroom, where she barfed and moaned while her mother attempted to give her a glass of bicarbonate of soda.

"She must have sneaked some booze into her room," Mr. Domínguez claimed, an indignant front disguising the amusement at the corners of his mouth.

Though I assured him we hadn't, he said my face had a sickly green tinge to it. He insisted Mrs. Domínguez prepare a dose of the same medicine for me. When we got up the next morning, Susie and I were afraid to touch the omelet Mrs. Domínguez cooked for us. I finally dug in. My appetite in the morning was stronger than my concerns about a new bout of indigestion.

The two days before the start of school seemed to last forever. I planned different hairstyles and tried on new shades of lipstick, until Mami grew worried about the number of times I washed my hair and face. I grew anxious with anticipation. I could hardly wait for the day to arrive. I didn't remember feeling this way about returning to school since I was in first grade, when attending school raised my status to "big girl."

When the day finally arrived, I stepped out of the house in my new black outfit, wearing a little white T-shirt under the jacket and my hair in perfect condition. I strapped my backpack over one shoulder and carried the shopping bag, with the pressed tablecloth in it, in the other hand. I skipped down the front steps and started down the sidewalk.

Then, to my surprise, I noticed I was holding a jasmine between my fingers. I had grown so used to picking one every morning, the habit had become automatic. My first reaction was to drop it. My feelings for Zach had changed. In fact, the mention of his name no longer made me shiver with excitement. It made me shudder. But instead of letting it drop, I brought the blossom to my nose and took in the sweet scent.

Before I knew it, I was plucking the petals, one at a time and calling out the usual chant: *loves me, loves me not*. But the picture in my mind was not of the blond basketball player. My heart lurched, sending a tremor of excitement through me. I was plucking the petals for Justin. Memories raced through my

151

mind, of moments together when he was thoughtful and gentle. My feelings for him spiraled, until I thought I'd burst with delight.

When the last petal was left, I resisted plucking it. I called out the most gratifying words I'd heard in days: *He loves me!* I saved the remains of the flower in the pocket of my jacket. But I remember little else about my hike to school. I think I floated all the way there.

"You look sharp!" Susie exclaimed, standing in the school hallway by my locker, where we'd arranged to meet. "I hope you're going to let me borrow the skirt and jacket."

I set down the shopping bag and wriggled free of my backpack. "Look what I got!" I told her excitedly, reaching into my pocket.

Susie looked dismayed when I brought out the remains of the jasmine, which had now turned a sickly shade of brown. "You're not back to holding out hope. The guy's not worth it, Maggie. I thought you'd rid yourself of him."

"Forget Zach!" I laughed, genuinely freed. "This jasmine was for . . ." I searched behind me cautiously, then I whispered, "It was for Justin. It said he loved me."

Susie threw up her hands. "You didn't need a flower to tell you that, *chica.* I told you Justin was crazy about you!"

A rush of heat traveled over my cheeks as I slipped the jasmine quickly into my pocket. "Shh! You're gonna let the whole world in on this!"

Susie looked around, then said as loud as ever, "There's no one around. At least none of Justin's friends."

I clamped my hand over my heart. "I swear, Susie. If word gets back to him . . ."

"Why are you so concerned all of a sudden about what Justin might think?" She watched me from the corner of her eye and gave me a playful smile. "Could it be he's finally gotten to you?"

I bit my lip and dipped my head slightly.

"Hah! I knew it!" Her voice rocked with laughter. "I knew Justin would win your heart!"

"¡Cállate, Susie!" I hissed. "Shut up!" My cheeks and ears steamed from embarrassment. "If he hears you, I'll die!"

"No, you won't. I have a feeling Justin would be happy to hear about it." Susie took the shopping bag. "Let's put the table-cloth in the locker so we can walk around before school starts."

I stored the bag and my lunch in the small metal box and took out the books I needed. Then, we strolled down the hall as a few of the students began to mingle, waiting for the first bell. "So, how do I fix things now? How do I let Justin know I changed my mind about him?"

"It's going to be tough. I could've asked Carlos to talk to Justin, but I'll never speak to Carlos again." Susie shook her head. "I can't believe you told Justin there was someone else. You really blew it."

"Thanks." My words were drenched in sarcasm. "I really needed to hear that."

"Sorry." Susie seemed to be in deep thought for a moment. "I guess you can talk to him. You know, be sweet and stuff. I think boys are able to tell when there's a flame burning."

I studied her from the corner of my eye. "Maybe you can talk to him."

Susie stopped. "Don't ask me to do that. I don't want to get involved. Carlos will think I want us to get back together."

I pressed my lips. "I understand."

"Ask him to join us for lunch. I'll save us a table."

"Okay." I gave her an unsure smile. "I'll try to get up the nerve. I'll see you then."

I caught a glimpse of Justin while changing classes. He wore a denim work shirt and dark gray pants that made him appear taller and more muscular than I remembered. My pulse fluttered wildly. I smiled and waved. But he didn't seem to notice me, though I was sure I caught his eye. I watched until he vanished in the crowd of students.

Zach walked into German class and searched around for me. Though I hadn't planned to save him a seat, out of habit, the other kids left the desk to my right vacant for him. He spotted me and nodded. My lips broke into a confident smile, as I realized my insides didn't tingle.

"Good thing you saved me a place," he told me, straddling the seat. "I've got to start off the year right in German."

"What do you think of the outfit?" I asked him boldly. A couple of weeks back, I would have cuddled a warty toad rather than get up the nerve to ask his opinion of my looks.

Zach checked me out, top to bottom. "It's nice. Is it new?"

"Duh! It was your family's Christmas present."

He chuckled. "I don't remember things like that."

"Listen, I have something to give you. Can you meet me at my locker after school? That way you don't have to carry it around all day."

"What is it?"

We waited for the sharp clanging of the bell to stop. But before I could answer, he smiled, a smug glint in his eyes. "I know. You got me a late Christmas present."

I snorted disdainfully. "Yeah, right!"

When I left German class, I looked around anxiously for Justin. I'd run into him before at this hour. His next class was close to Mr. Sutter's geometry class. Though I walked slowly, I arrived at Mr. Sutter's door without spotting him. I put my books on my desk and ran out the door, pretending to be desperate for a drink of water. As I leaned over the fountain, I saw Justin coming my way. I straightened up and waited for him to draw closer.

My breath caught in my throat and I prayed my voice wouldn't crack. "Hi! Did you have a nice vacation?"

For a moment, our eyes met. A quiver of excitement swished through me.

But he broke the eye contact and stared straight ahead. Without a break in his pace, he answered me. "Yeah. It was fine."

He didn't say another word. He never looked back. I watched him blend into the crowd, my ego wilting like sun-parched lettuce.

I listened to Mr. Sutter's discussion of the day's lesson, surprised that, for once, geometry made sense to me. I pictured the pool table in Justin's family room. I remembered how he taught me to measure with the stick the angles required to hit the balls just right. I finally could relate what I'd learned in geometry class to a real-world experience. I was understanding the lecture. Justin had been right. Math was just a series of puzzles to be solved. Justin had been right about a lot of things.

At lunch, Susie was saving a table for me in the patio. I sat across from her, leaving my lunch bag and soda untouched.

"Well?" she asked.

"Well what?" I answered her, my voice flat and lifeless, though I had a hunch I knew what she meant.

"Did you ask Justin to meet us for lunch?"

I propped my chin on my hands. "No."

Susie popped the tab on her can of Coke. "Did you get cold feet?" She took a slug.

"He didn't give me a chance." I sighed. "He kept right on walking when I tried to start a conversation."

She examined the ripples in a potato chip. "During a change in class?"

I nodded.

"He was probably in a hurry." Susie shrugged, crunching on the salty morsel. "I'm always rushing between classes."

I lowered my eyes. "I don't think that was his problem."

"Well, you can't give up after one try." Susie took a bite of her sandwich. "Chicken salad. Want a bite?"

I shook my head.

"You've got to eat, *chica*. What's in your bag?" She took out my ham sandwich, the bag of chips, then suddenly stopped before she found the brownies I'd packed. Her face paled. "There he is," she whispered.

My heart hammered in my chest. I wasn't sure what I'd do when I ran into Justin again. "Who?"

"Carlos," she said, breathlessly. "It looks like he's heading out for fast food with some friends."

I followed the group with my eyes. Justin wasn't among them. "Are you sorry Carlos didn't stop to say hello?"

Susie bit her lip. "I think it's for the best. I don't want someone around who's not looking out for me."

"But it hurt," I said softly.

"Well, to tell you the truth, it still hurts," Susie admitted.

I was sorry things hadn't worked out well for Susie. I knew her well enough to know Carlos' behavior had hurt her deeply. I was proud of her for sticking up for herself.

"Uh-oh. There comes the other one," she said, her lips hardly moving.

My insides jangled. I leaned forward. "Justin?"

She nodded without taking her eyes off him. "Go ask him to sit with you."

"I'm scared! I can't do it."

"Yes, you can. He still likes you. The jasmine proved it this morning. Besides, you can't get a person out of your system in just a few days. Believe me, Maggie."

"I did it!" I reminded her. "I managed to get Zach out of my life just like that." I snapped my fingers in front of her face.

"That's because he treated you rotten."

"What makes you think Justin didn't shake me off the same way? I didn't give him much hope either."

"It's different with Justin. I see it in the way he looks at you. I think he cares for you in a different way."

"Do you really think so?"

Susie swatted my hands, which were laced together on the table, as if in prayer. "Go after him, *chica*, before he gets away. *¡Vé!*"

I bolted from the table without thinking, emboldened by Susie's assurances. Justin was rounding a corner, heading back into the school building. I scurried after him.

"Justin! Hold up. I want to talk to you."

He glanced at me and waited.

"Hi!" I managed to say, feeling stupid.

"Hi." His face was icy.

"Susie and I have a table outside. I thought you might want, you know, to sit with us."

He didn't blink an eye. "I've got other plans."

I could feel the blood drain from my face.

"I'm sure you prefer some other company," he muttered as he turned to go.

My insides withered in pain. "What was that?" I wasn't sure I'd heard him right. I couldn't accept that he didn't care for me anymore. Not after he'd won me over.

"Never mind," he answered as he walked away.

I slunk back to Susie, with tears rimming my eyes. "It's over. I really blew it."

"I can't figure him out," Susie said, shaking her head. "I was so sure he still cared about you . . ."

"It's my own fault." I dropped down on my seat. "I shut him out of my life."

Returning the tablecloth to Zach had lost much of the importance it had carried for days. Though I was still interested in showing him that I'd met his challenge, I now had another disappointment to take over my thoughts. I went from class to class in a daze. In the span of a school day, I had both discovered love and lost it.

Zach was leaning on the bank of lockers waiting when I arrived.

"What've you got for me?" He gave me a crooked grin that would have sent my heart skittering weeks ago.

I started turning the dial on the lock. "It's really something I want you to give your mother."

His grin washed away like a stain. "Oh, that thing."

"The tablecloth," I specified.

"Is it okay? I'd hate to be the one to bring her the bad news."

"See for yourself," I said struggling with the combination.

"Oh, give me that." Zach took the lock in his hands. He turned the dial as I called out the numbers. In a moment he had the locker open.

I handed him the shopping bag. "It's spotless."

"I've been looking for you all over the place!" Kelly Rogers said, rushing toward us. "Where have you been?"

"I had to meet Maggie. She wanted to give me something." He kneed the shopping bag. "Do you know Maggie?"

Kelly gave me quick leer. "I don't think so." The girl's high-pitched voice rattled me.

"Maggie's in my German class."

I noticed he didn't ask me if I'd met her and he didn't bother to introduce us.

Kelly's eyes glowed with impatience.

I had little else to say to him. I snapped the lock back in place and turned to go.

"I'll surprise you sometime and stop by Grams," Zach said, with a cocky wink. But now I was sure his words were meant to rile Kelly rather than encourage me.

"I'm there everyday," I said, walking away.

"Hey, listen," he said, raising the shopping bag by the handles. "Thanks."

"Sure. And thanks for your Christmas present, too." I pinched the cloth of the black jacket to draw attention to it. He was trying to raise his stock in Kelly's presence. But I knew how to play the game, too.

I heard Kelly's whine as I rounded the corner of the hallway, and I stopped to listen, out of their sight. "You gave her a Christmas present?" the girl hissed. "A black denim jacket?"

I bit my lip to suppress a giggle. I wouldn't miss a word for a year's pay.

"My sister picked it out. I had nothing to do with it."

"Your sister picked out the present you gave her?"

"It wasn't a gift from me, Kelly. It was from the whole family. Maggie came over to my house for Christmas."

"You had her over to your house? For Christmas?" she asked, incredulous.

"My family knows her. That's all." The picture of droplets of sweat welling up on his brow brought a smile to my face. "Come on, Kelly. Give me a break."

Her voice grew louder. "So, she handed you her Christmas present at school."

"This isn't a present. She's returning something to my mother."

"I can't believe this!" Her voice rose to a furious pitch. I covered my mouth, afraid they'd hear the giggles gushing from my throat. "She borrowed something from your mother?"

"No, Kelly. She didn't borrow it. It's my mother's fancy tablecloth. Maggie got some stains on it from some *Cuban* dish she brought to our house. She took it home to wash it."

My heart skipped a beat. Zach had put all the blame for what happened on me. He wasn't owning up to any responsibility. I gritted my teeth in anger.

"Why would she do that?" I pictured Kelly's eyes narrowing with suspicion.

"I don't know," Zach said. "I guess she and her mother know how to get things clean. You see, she works for my grandmother."

"You mean Maggie's mother is her Cuban maid?" Kelly asked.

"No, not her mother," Zach said. "*Maggie's* my grandmother's maid."

My legs softened like soup noodles. I leaned against the wall for support. Is that how he viewed my work for his grandmother? I was looking out for Mrs. Maxwell's health. That's what Dr. Stevens had recommended. That's why he'd turned to my mother, a nurse, for a reference. That's what Mrs. Maxwell was paying me for.

I gasped for air through my gaping mouth. But it didn't stop the shaking in my limbs. And it didn't slow down the tears that welled in my eyes. I clutched my backpack and bounded down the empty hall, flanked by a speeding watery blur of multi-colored metal lockers and closed classroom doors.

The heavy gate to the parking lot gave way to my powerful shove as easily as if it'd been the door to a birdcage. A few kids still hanging around on the street stared. I must have been a sight, with tears streaming down my cheeks and a canvas backpack banging heavily against my side as I ran.

"Maggie, wait for me!" Conchi tried to catch up, her chubby legs moving fast as I'd ever seen. "*¿Qué te pasa?*"

I waved her away. I wasn't in the mood to explain things to her.

At first, my only interest was to get away from the building, to put some distance between me and the creep Zach had turned out to be. I ran without destination. I couldn't show up at Mrs.

Maxwell's house convulsing with fury and humiliation. I was supposed to help her, not the other way around. Besides, she'd want to know the cause of my misery and I could never bring myself to tell the poor lady how rotten her grandson was. As comforting as it would be to bury my face in my pillow, that was also out of the question. Susie was intent on finding out how things went after school. If I didn't answer the phone, she might show up at my house. I felt too miserable to have company. I dashed to Lowe Grove Park, halfway between school and home.

There, I took over a wooden bench half hidden by a bush and, covering my face with my hands, gave in to the painful sobs I'd held back. The first day back to school had proven to be a disaster. I'd devoted so much attention to Zach the last few weeks unaware he'd had so little regard for me. I had wasted so much time. I had been such a fool.

I had finally realized that Justin was a worthwhile friend. Not only that, I'd fallen for him. And I could only blame myself for losing him. I unbuttoned the top pocket of my jacket and drew out the wilted, one-petaled jasmine from the morning. I had counted on the jasmine again. And again, it had misled me. I let it drop from my hand and watched it land on the sandy jogging trail.

I cried for a few minutes, then began to compose myself. I dug in my backpack for tissues and blew my nose. My hands were covered with runny mascara, and I figured my cheeks were streaked with black marks. I spotted a jogger coming down the path, so I searched in my bag for another tissue. I wanted to wipe my face before even a stranger passed by and saw me like this.

"Maggie, are you crying? What's wrong?"

At the sound of his voice, my jaw dropped as if it was chiseled out of granite. The jogger was Justin. I swallowed hard to force my thumping heart back down to my chest. Justin was the last person I'd want to see me in this condition.

I grabbed the tissue and tried to rub my face dry. "Nothing," I groaned. As much as I tried to collect myself, my answer was followed by an agonizing sob.

He dropped down beside me on the bench. I could hear his labored breathing, though I didn't have the nerve to look up at him. I grabbed the tissue and tried to rub my face dry.

"Something's wrong. Tell me what happened."

I shook my head. To my consternation, his concern brought fresh tears to my eyes.

Justin was quiet for a moment. Leaning forward, he rested his elbows on his knees and laced his hands together. "It's because I shot you down at school today, isn't it?"

My eyes flashed open in panic. I couldn't tell him that was part of it. He'd realize I cared about him. I wouldn't admit to that, when he no longer had feelings for me.

"If it is, I'm sorry I hurt you."

I dabbed my eyes with the tissue. "It's something else."

"It's someone else, you mean," he said, with an assertive tilt of his head.

I sighed. "Yes."

Justin took a deep breath. "What did he do?"

"He said something that hurt me."

"You must care a lot about him." A muscle in his jaw quivered.

"No, I don't. Really."

"Come on, Maggie." His lips thinned with impatience. "Words don't hurt unless the person means something to you."

"Well, I used to care about him, I'll admit. But I don't anymore." The tissue was a ragged ball in my hands. "What hurt was to find out how little respect he had for me."

From the corner of my eye, I saw his hands tighten into fists. "Did he try to do something stupid? 'Cause if he did . . ."

I concealed the twinge of hope that came to life inside me. "No, it was nothing like that. I don't think he knew I could hear him. He was talking to someone else about me and my job. I take care of an older lady after school, you know."

"I remember."

"Well, Mrs. Maxwell is Zach's grandmother."

"And Zach's the jerk you've got the hots for." The corner of his mouth took on a cynical twist.

I threw my hands up. "He's not important to me anymore. I told you already."

He ignored my frustration. "So what about your job?"

"His grandmother broke her leg last summer and her daughter wanted someone to look in on her. Her doctor was a friend of my dad's and he asked my mom if I'd take the job. He said he'd give me a good reference for nursing school, because it would be a related experience."

"So you broke the lady's other leg and she fired you." His face split into a teasing smile. I got a peek at the tight muscles of his chest through wide armhole of his tank top.

"That's not funny, Justin." In spite of my effort to resist, I found myself giggling.

His clear green eyes sparkled as he watched me, sending a distracting wave of delight down my spine. "You're right," he said, getting serious again.

I shifted uneasily on the bench, then drew up the courage to repeat the offending words. "Zach told his girlfriend that I was his grandmother's Cuban maid."

I studied Justin's face for a sympathetic reaction. There was only a vague questioning in his eyes.

"So?"

"I'm not there to clean her house," I shouted, my temper flaring when he didn't support my indignation. "I'm there to make sure she's healthy!"

"Everyone else knows that," Justin said calmly. "What do you care what the jerk thinks?"

"He said it to demean me, Justin." I searched his face for a sign of compassion. "His girlfriend was jealous of me. He put me down to make her feel better."

"Maggie." Justin leaned back on the bench and locked his gaze on me. I stared straight ahead, afraid to meet his eyes. I could feel my cheeks glowing with heat. "What does that tell you about the guy?"

I was silent for a moment, my concentration torn to bits by his steady gaze. Finally, I tilted my head in a nod. "He's a user. He's shallow and self-absorbed. He's a creep."

He held out his hands palms up, like the pages of an open book. "Steer away from people like that, Maggie. Hang around people who are friends."

"I know that now."

He waved a hand in dismissal and blew an exasperated huff. "And forget that jerk!"

His persistence about my feelings for Zach irked me. "I don't care about him anymore! I care about someone else!" I was as surprised by my admission as Justin was.

"Great," he said, in an icy voice.

I was immobile with shock. Justin had misunderstood. I had dared to hint at my feelings for him and now he thought I liked some other guy.

He swatted the side of his leg impatiently. "Well, I gotta go."

A knot of alarm tightened in my chest as he rose from the bench. "You don't understand."

"I get the message all right, Maggie."

"No, you don't," I replied, rising from the bench and cutting off his path. In spite of the disappointments I'd suffered in the day, I had to take a chance. *Go for it, Maggie. Don't blow it again.* "What I meant to say was that I like *you!*"

Justin stopped cold. He pivoted and scratched his head, confusion and delight working slowly across his face. "You mean—? You mean—?"

I couldn't help the nervous burst of giggles that accompanied my answer. "Yes, that's what I mean!"

"Damn! Maggie!" he said, slapping his thigh.

I held my breath. "What's wrong?"

He cocked his head to one side and a smile of surprise tipped the corners of his mouth. He enveloped me in his arms. "Nothing. Nothing at all. Everything's great!"

It was funny to kiss and laugh at the same time. His lips were moist and the contact with his teeth sent a tingle of delight down my spine.

He brushed the hair from my face. "You're beautiful."

"Oh, Justin. Don't make fun of me. I bet I look like a clown with make-up running down my face."

He placed the tip of his finger on my nose. "And a red, puffy nose."

We laughed happily in each other's arms. I dropped my chin on his chest, enjoying the feel of his lanky arms around me. I was amazed to see my dejection and misery transform in seconds to a heady joy.

The jasmine had been right after all. It hadn't misled me. I reached down and delicately pinched between my fingers the remains of the jasmine I had dropped. It was brown and withered, but to me, it had suddenly become a cherished jewel.

"What's that?" Justin asked.

I gave him a slight shrug. "A jasmine from my vine. I know it looks pretty shriveled, but this one I'm saving."

Justin smiled, though I wasn't sure he understood. "Come on, my car's back here. I'll take you home."

"I have to check in on Mrs. Maxwell."

"Okay. We'll stop by your house so you can wash your face and then I'll drop you off at her house."

As we drove up, Mrs. Maxwell was watering the angel-wing begonia we had transferred to the front porch. I was glad there was no trace of the weeping on my face. I'd looked in the mirror after I splashed my face clean and saw only a radiant glow.

"Hello, Maggie." She waved as I approached, with Justin coming up behind me. "I'm so glad to see you didn't have to walk. It's so warm for January . . ."

"Hi," I replied. "This is my friend Justin."

Justin bounded up the steps and offered Mrs. Maxwell a firm grip.

"Justin, this is Mrs. Maxwell."

"Justin Bentley," he said. "Nice to meet you."

"Glad to meet a friend of Maggie's. She's a wonderful girl." Mrs. Maxwell put an arm around me and squeezed me. I gave Justin a shy smile. "I look forward to her company every day."

"You should wait for me to take care of the plants," I said, taking the watering can from her hand. "The can's too heavy."

She winked a clear blue eye at Justin. "See what I mean?"

Justin nodded and grinned.

"Do you go to Glades Ridge with Maggie?"

"I sure do. I'm a sophomore."

"I hope you're doing well in your studies."

"I am. I keep up my grades so I'll get into a good college. I'm going to be an engineer, like my dad."

I shot him a quizzical look. I wondered if he'd come to that conclusion on his own, without his father's push.

He cocked his head and nodded at me.

"There's a responsible young man!" Mrs. Maxwell exclaimed. "I wish that other young men your age were as level-headed."

Justin chuckled, his teeth glinting in the afternoon brightness. I was sure he'd understood she was referring to Zach.

"I'd better get going," he said. "It was nice to meet you."

"It was a pleasure," Mrs. Maxwell said.

"I'll stop by your house tonight. Is that all right, Maggie?"

My heart leaped with anticipation. "Great! I'll see you tonight."